Candy Cotton Café

By Lola

ISBN-10: 0-9981297-2-0

ISBN-13: 978-0-9981297-2-3

Dedication

To my husband, Larry, who has taken on the difficult task of being my assistant. I dedicate this book to a long list of family and friends with love. I appreciate their loving encouragement, support and patience.

My precious daughters and grandchildren will always be my loving inspiration.

A Special Thanks To:

Mary W. for being my longtime extended family and prayer partner.

Sandra K. for her role in helping me bravely follow my heart. She has provided me with new strength to fulfill my life's journey.

Shannon C. for being my friend. She consistently gives me loving support and encouraging words. She's encouraged me and given me hope to fulfill my book-writing dreams.

Tammy G. for being my longtime friend and my Dream Team Partner.

Preface

My story, 'Candy Cotton Café', is based on pure fiction created from my imagination. All my fictional characters' names and the names of my fictional places were chosen via my imagination. Any name that is the same of a real person or place is strictly a coincidence. My fiction story is about love, romance, family and adventure. It's intended to be an easy read for both young and old.

Ordinarily, when one has car trouble on the highway, they're not happy about it. While driving home from a business trip, Jake's car breaks down on the highway. His auto service directs the tow truck driver to deliver it to a mechanic in the closest town. The tow truck driver indeed delivers Jake's car to 'Al's Auto Repair Shop' in a town which is known as Happiness.

The mechanic, Al, is not able to fix the car without a special part that he must order. Jake asks Al to suggest a place to get a good meal and a place to stay overnight. Al loans him a car but his trip home is still several hours away. Al suggests the 'Candy Cotton Café' which is located a couple of blocks down the street. The food is always fresh and delicious. You won't find better service anywhere. He also suggests the 'Cotton Family Bed & Breakfast, known as the B&B, is a great place to stay overnight.

Jake is very tired and hungry. He checks out the café and meets Candance Cotton, the owner of the Café. She introduces him to her Aunt Jenny who owns the Bed and Breakfast. It's a Thursday night and he's anxious to be home with his son, David. Meeting Candy and her family turns out to be an exciting new adventure in Happiness. This weekend will prove to be life-changing for them.

Table of Content

Chapter One
I'm Delighted

Howdy, my name is Candace Cotton. You can call me Candy. My youngest brother was two and a half years old when he tried to say Candace. His attempt created my nickname which stuck like glue. I was taunted from kindergarten through my college years with classmates calling me "Cotton Candy".

I own the Candy Cotton Café located on the corner of Main and Walnut in my small country town, Happiness, USA. The town didn't get its name because everyone is happy. The founder of this town hoped people would find happiness here.

My Aunt Jenny, also known as Jen, is my assistant manager of this cafe. We just finished serving up meals from behind the deli and bakery counter. I'm tackling the aftermath of the lunch crowd wearing a blue dress with white apron. My long hair is tucked under a cap. Aunt Jen is scurrying over to the wall to answer the business phone.

She's a little short of breath but routinely says, "Candy Cotton Café. How can I help you?"

While hunched over picking up a receipt that I dropped on the floor, I see a tall, handsome and mysterious looking stranger. I watch while he stands outside the front door peering through my shop window. He's wearing a fancy business suit. It really stands out amongst the residents of this small town. Casual dress is the norm for our country folks around here.

What this mystery man sees, is a mystery to him. He sees a young lady in a blue dress with a white apron. She's hunched over and working behind a counter. He can't see her face but takes note of her beautiful golden hair peeking out of her cap. The older lady by the wall talking on the phone is also wearing a blue dress with a white apron. He can't see her face either but notices a sparkle from a gold chain hanging around her neck and dangling from her glasses. As he scans the room, the red round top bar stools are obvious. They match the red round seats on the chairs by the small round tables.

He looks above the door and reads the sign, 'Candy Cotton Café'. When he's sure this is the correct establishment, he turns the doorknob and enters. Hesitating, he scans the room to learn more about this new place. His car broke down out on the highway while passing through this town. The tow truck driver picked up his car and dropped it off at a repair shop just down the street. The mechanic can't make the repairs today. He suggested Candy Cotton Café for a place to eat a meal. He also suggested a bed and breakfast for a place to sleep overnight. Fortunately, the mechanic loaned him an old car to get around town during his stay here.

He steps up to the counter and reads a sign advertising today's special. The clock on the wall displays three fifteen. It's too late for lunch and too early for dinner. The special sounds refreshing to this hungry man. He's a little surprised to see Lox on the menu at a small-town café.

I greet him with a smile and ask, "How can I help you? May I take your order?"

In a deep voice, he replies, "Do you know the mechanic, Al, at the auto repair shop? He told me to tell you that he sent me here. The bakery and deli special for today looks tasty. I think I'll try the lox."

I'm feeling a little giddy but in a muffled flat tone, I say, "The locks? Oh, they're working fine."

He chuckles and gives her a little wink and a smile. "Ah, good one! Just what I needed to help relieve the stress of my day."

I smile and ask, "Would you like a beverage with your order? Would you like tomato or capers as a topping?'

He replied, "Both tomato and capers will taste great. I'm hungry. I'm also very thirsty after a long road trip. I'll take a large glass of the iced sweet tea. Thank you, Candy. That is the name on your name tag, right? My name is Jacob but my friends call me Jake."

I respond, "Yes, my name is Candy, Candy Cotton. I'm delighted to make your acquaintance, Jacob. I'll be right back with your order. If you want to sit at a table and relax, I can serve your meal to you there."

"Sounds great, thanks again, Candy. I'm glad to meet you, too. I'll just take a seat by the window at a table in the corner."

He sits down but he can't relax. His cell phone is filled with voicemail and texts from both his business associates and his family back home. While he's waiting for his meal, he takes time to read the texts.

I prepare his order using a fresh baked bagel from the bakery in the café. The salmon, tomato and capers are fresh from the deli. I serve the fresh sour cream in a small serving bowl. There's a place setting on the table. Aunt Jen helps fill this order by pouring fresh brewed sweet tea over ice in a large glass. I place his food neatly on a tray. Aunt Jen carries the glass of tea over to his table and places it on a coaster. I carry the tray and place his plate with the lox on the table in front of him.

He's preoccupied with his cell phone because he's listening to voicemail messages. He looks up and smiles at both. He nods and says, "Thank you!"

I don't want to disturb him but softly I say, "Let me know if I can do anything else for you."

"This is great! Everything is fine." He turns off his phone and enjoys his meal in a quiet and relaxed atmosphere. His mind is still preoccupied with the car problems as well as multiple business and family concerns.

Jen and I walk away and continue our work behind the counter. We anticipate our usual dinner crowd around five or five-thirty. We keep busy with to-go orders as well as the people eating-in our little café. We work hard and have maintained a five-star reputation. Our food is always fresh and their service is superb. The waiter who runs the coffee bar will arrive soon to prepare for the dinner crowd. Also, a waitress and a busboy, who is also our dishwasher, are on their way.

I check in with him offering to clear the table which will give him more space to work. I ask, "Because you're new to our town, would you like a free sample of our fresh baked apple pie?"

Jacob replies, "That's a generous offer. I would love to eat a slice of apple pie. I, also, need a cup of hot strong coffee to help me stay awake. Do you have a cup of coffee that you can serve with the pie? I've got lots of work to do but I feel stressed and tired." He smiles with gratitude. "Do you have a minute to sit and visit with me? I have several questions that need answers. I've never been here before and I'm feeling a little lost."

I respond, "Sure thing. I'm not expecting any customers for a while. My Aunt Jen can handle any customers that come in while we chat. I'll be right back with your pie and coffee."

He gets up and goes out to retrieve his briefcase from the car. When he returns to his table, I'm standing by and waiting with the hot coffee and apple pie. He asks, "Would you like to sit down for our chat and relax for a few minutes?"

I reply, "Okay, at best, I have a few minutes." I gently sit down on a chair across the table from him. I find myself gazing into his beautiful hazel eyes. At the same time, he's looking deeply into my blue eyes. We pause. It seems we're mutually feeling a friendly connection."

He shares, "Al not only suggested I visit your café for a meal but he suggested The Cotton Family B&B for an overnight stay. Is the Cotton Family B&B (Bed & Breakfast) related to you or your family?"

"Yes, my Aunt Jenny owns the B&B and runs the business in her large house. Her niece and I also live in her house with her. She helps me out here when she can and I help her at her B&B when needed. Her niece helps with household chores and general housesitting while she's away. Are you needing a room there for the night? I'll send Aunt Jenny over to talk to you."

I walk back behind the counter and realize Aunt Jenny is in the business office at the back. When we meet in the hallway, I tell her, "Jacob is a potential B&B customer. Al won't be able to repair Jacob's car today. Al suggested your B&B for an overnight stay. He has questions that need answers." I smile lovingly at my Aunt Jen who I admire tremendously. She's a very dedicated and hard worker trying to make ends meet for their survival.

Aunt Jenny says, "Okay, I'll go speak with him. The timing is good right now. Will you be able to watch the counters?"

My answer is, "Yes, of course!" I'm able to see and hear the happenings in the café. I watch Aunt Jen and Jacob as they communicate. I overhear her tell him, "We can meet at the B&B and I can show you your room before you pay. What time is convenient? If it's after the dinner crowd, I can give you a tour. Otherwise, my niece, Darla Cunningham, can assist you there."

He says, I don't want to cause anyone any trouble. I can wait until after the dinner hour if you prefer. I'll just go outside and walk around on this beautiful day. I'll return here for dinner after the rush hour. The food and hospitality here is great. Thanks for making me feel welcome in your café and in this town. I've found a little happiness here despite my car and business troubles."

Aunt Jenny says, "I hope you enjoy your walk and your stay in our little town. I'll talk to you later then." She hands him a piece of paper that has the address and map giving directions to her B&B.

"Thank you, Ms. Cotton. On second thought, I'll drive out there to see the building and surrounding area while it's still daylight. I prefer searching in daylight for a new place rather than getting lost in the darkness of night."

"You can call me Jenny. The people in this town are friendly. Candy said your name is Jacob, right? I'm delighted to meet you."

He replies, "Yes, my name is Jacob but my friends call me by my nickname, Jake. You can call me Jake. I'm happy to meet you, too. I'm going to leave here now but I'll see you later." He leaves a generous tip, picks up his briefcase and walks out the door. He waves goodbye in my direction. I smile and wave goodbye to him in return.

Jacob gets in his car and studies the map. He starts the car and is on his way to hunt for the Cotton Family Bed & Breakfast. The directions lead him down a country road that has several twists and turns like an old cow trail. When he arrives, he's in awe of this beautiful spacious house and the land surrounding it. There's a beautiful sparking lake with a sandy beach and a fishing pier. The B&B looks more like a vacation resort than an overnight stay with a free breakfast.

It's a beautiful day and he feels drawn to walk down to the edge of the lake. He's impressed by the beautiful stately trees that are on the property. He parks his car and starts walking in that direction. A beautiful golden collie barks at him but Jake stretches out his hand to greet her. There's a tag dangling from the dog's collar. He reads the name out loud. He says, "Lacey" and laughs. He pats the dog on her head and says, "I'm delighted to meet you!"

Chapter Two
Cotton Family B&B

Jake is down on one knee petting Lacey. She's obviously delighted to meet him. Her tail is wagging and swishing in the happiest way. He hears a lady's voice in the distance calling, "Laaaacey, Laaacey! Come here girl!

Darla appears from around the corner of the house. She's not sure what to make of this mysterious looking man. She believes that Lacey is a good judge of character. She says under her breath, "If Lacey trusts him, I guess I can, too."

She looks at him a little closer and wonders if this is the potential customer for the B&B. Aunt Jen called her from the café to give her a heads-up about a mysterious man who's new in town. Jake stands up and strolls toward her with Lacey walking right by his side.

When they meet, Jake extends his hand to greet her. He says, "Hello, my name is Jacob. Are you Jenny Cotton's niece, Darla?"

She replies, "Yes, I am. Aunt Jenny called to tell me you might drive by to find our B&B." She extends her hand and gently places it in his for a brief friendly handshake. "I wasn't expecting you to stop in."

He says, "My plan was to drive out and locate the Cotton Family B&B while it's still daylight. I wasn't planning to stop until I observed the awesome beauty. I parked with a desire to see more of the sparkling lake and beach. I've never seen anything like this before."

She says, "Welcome to our B&B and please feel free to walk out to the beach. It's a beautiful day. The fresh air here is energizing. I've got to take Lacey back into the house. I have work to do before Aunt Jen returns home tonight, too. We have a deck with chairs if you want to just sit and relax for a few. She told me you were planning to eat supper at the Candy Cotton Café tonight. Oh, would you like something to drink? Water? Tea? A soft drink?"

"No, thank you, I'm fine. I won't stay long. I would enjoy the walk by the lake and a chance to relax on the deck. Thank you so much for your hospitality. I think I'm going to like it here. Is it possible to rent a room for more than one night? Say, like for the upcoming weekend? The mechanic says he can fix my car tomorrow. I haven't had a vacation in a long time. Staying here for a weekend would be a great escape from the big city and its woes."

"I'm not sure if the room is available. You'll have to discuss that with Aunt Jen. You'll find it's very peaceful here. I'll probably see you later. I've got to take care of a few things inside. Did you want a quick tour to see the room Aunt Jen rents? You'll see the kitchen area on the way."

"Yes, maybe for a brief moment because you offered. I don't want to detain you or prevent you from getting your work done."

"Okay, please follow me." They walk up the steps of the deck and enter the back door. The kitchen is huge and has a nice setup for their guests. They walk up the staircase to the second floor. This huge house has high ceilings which adds to the ambience. They stop in front of a door and Darla pulls a keyring from her pocket. She unlocks and opens the door wide for Jake to see inside.

Jake says with great excitement, 'WOW! This room is impressive and I see it has an attached bathroom. This is by far better than any motel or hotel room that I've stayed in. My business requires me to travel often on the road   Oh, the view of the lake from this window is wonderful. Can I open this door and view it from the balcony?"

"Yes. We think it's a highlight of the room for our guest. They can sit out and see the stars as well as breathing in this clean fresh air. We had the balconies added when we decided to use our house for a B&B. What do you think?"

"I think it's perfect. I'm very excited about a chance to spend time where it's quiet and relaxing. It's very peaceful. Thank you, Darla, for your kindness and taking time for the tour. I'll leave you now. I'll walk down to the lake for a closer look and then I'll make my way back to the Café. I can see myself out."

"You're welcome, Jacob. I'm happy you like our B&B. I'll see you later."

Jacob walks down the stairs and pats Lacey on the head before walking out the back door. He stops on the deck for just a second to inhale the fresh air. He walks down to the beach and out to the end of the fishing pier. It's really a beautiful sight to see. The blue sky with the sunlight reflecting and sparkles on the water are mesmerizing. He recalls childhood memories of fishing with his Grandpa. It's been a long time since he's held a fishing pole and caught a fish. These are happy memories.

He walks back to the car and finds his camera. He proceeds to take several pictures of the house, lake and trees for a keepsake of his visit in Happiness. He uses the map and directions that Jenny gave him to find his way back to the Candy Cotton Café.

When he arrives at the diner, he sees that it's very busy. He must find a parking spot for the car on the side street. He's surprised to see a crowd and a flurry of activity in a café on a Thursday night. While resting his forehead on the steering wheel, he tries to decide what to do. He's not up to that much crowd and stress after the relaxing experience he had at the B&B. He decides to take a walk down Main St for a little exercise and stress relief.

After walking around like a tourist for a half hour, he notices the crowd in the Café has thinned out considerably. He bravely walks in but the jingle of the overhead bell gives him away. The people there have already heard the story about the new, mysterious, tall and handsome man in town. They take a quick look but all return to their conversations and eating their meals.

The Café is set up for the dinner meal and takes on a completely different appearance. There are red tablecloths instead of the paper placemats they use during the lunch hour. People wait to be seated and are ordering off a menu.

I watch Jake hunker down a little when the bell jingles. I know how overwhelming it feels when you try to fit in with strangers. My intuition tells me to seat him at the same table where he ate lunch with us earlier. Fortunately, the diners at that table just left. I personally walk over to the table to clear and wash it. He looks at me and smiles. I quickly rush to his side and lead him to his table. He sits down and sighs with relief.

I smile and say, "Hey, Jake. How are you doing? Here's a dinner menu. I'll check back with you for your order in a minute. We've all been busy here tonight. Would you like a beverage to drink while you wait? We don't serve alcohol here. I have the usual selection to choose from. Water? Tea? Coffee? Soft drinks? Fruit juice?"

I smile at him resting his elbow on the table with his chin on the palm of his hand. He looks up at me and says with a smile, "A glass of water would be great for now, thank you."

"You've got it. One glass of water coming right up." They both laugh. I walk away but I return in less than a minute. I place the tall glass of cold water on a coaster on the table. He's reading the menu but glances up long enough to say, "Thanks, Candy!"

I go back to work helping the crew take care of the diners in my Café. I watch out of the corner of my eye to be sure no one is being neglected. My waitress is standing by his table. They chat and laugh while she writes down his order on her ticket pad. I believe she'll take proper care of his dining needs. I double check his order and have a quick chat with my cook in the kitchen. My cook is excellent but I ask him to give a little extra attention to Jacob's order.

Business is slowing down and the café is quieter. Jacob is working on his cell phone and with something inside his open briefcase. I decide to do a walkthrough of the Café. I like to spot check all my tables and just to be sure my crew is doing their job properly. When I walk by Jake's table, our eyes meet and we exchange smiles. He still looks very mysterious.

I ask him, "How are things going here, Jake? I think your meal should be right out. Would you like a refill on the water?"

Jake replies, "I'm doing great. No, thank you. I ordered sweet tea with my meal."

"Glad to hear you're doing okay."

He closes his briefcase and puts his cell phone in his shirt's pocket. He asks, "If you have an extra minute, would you like to join me for a chat?"

"I have an extra minute right now. I haven't had a break since the beginning of our dinner rush. I'll get your glass of sweet tea and pour one for myself. I'll be right back."

I prepare two glasses of sweet tea and walk back to his table. The waitress is placing his meal on the table now. With a smile, I tell her, "Thank you!"

I set down the two glasses of tea on coasters. I ask, "Do you want to chat later? I want you to enjoy your meal while it's hot."

Jake replies, "If it's okay with you and you have the time, we can chat now."

I sit down on a chair across the table. I'm also keep an eye and ear open for my Café crew and diners. It was a great crowd for a Thursday night. The crowd has dispersed leaving a few people sitting at tables and on stools at the coffee bar. My crew is doing a great job. I feel relieved to sit down and relax with a glass of tea.

Jake says, "Thank you for joining me for a chat. I want to tell you, I'm impressed with your Café, the

B&B and the friendly people in this town. There's a feeling of peacefulness around here that I've never experienced in the big city."

"When my family moved to Happiness, we were searching for a peaceful place to live and work. We found our happiness and peace here in this community. I'm glad you had a chance to visit our town and experience the peacefulness and friendliness. Did you say you saw the B&B?"

"Yes, Aunt Jenny gave me a map with directions. I drove out there to see it while it's still daylight. What time does your Aunt leave here for her home and B&B?"

"The time varies. It depends on the work we must do after the doors are locked. She's in our office in the back. I'll let her know that you're here. She told me earlier that you two would meet here regarding a room for an overnight stay."

"Whenever she has the time, I'm interested in renting the room Darla showed me today. I hope it's available. It has a lovely view of the lake."

"Oh, you met my cousin, Darla?"

Jake responds, "Yes and the family dog, Lacey! I enjoyed my experience at the B&B today and I look forward to an overnight stay."

"I'll go talk to Aunt Jen and let her know that you're interested in renting the room." I stand up and clear the table of all empty dishes. I set them in the kitchen sink on my way to the office. I tap on the closed door and hear Aunt Jen say, "Come on in."

I tell her, "Jacob is interested in renting a room at the B&B tonight. He's waiting at the corner table in the cafe to talk to you."

"Oh, that's good news. Please tell him, I'll be right there. I'm happy that he wants to stay at our Cotton Family B&B."

Chapter Three
Happy Weekend

Jenny quickly completes her office responsibility and hurries out to talk to Jake. He's waiting patiently to speak with her about renting the room. She sits down across the table from him.

With a smile, she says, "Hi Jacob, I hope you you'll be able to find your way back to the B&B. Darla and I spoke after your visit there. She told me that you like the room she showed you today. It's available for the weekend."

He says, "Hi Jenny, I'm pretty sure that I can find your B&B again. It's very impressive."

"If you're serious about staying through the weekend, please meet me at the B&B in about a half hour. We can handle your registration and payment at my kitchen table."

He says, "Sounds great. I'll see you there. I'm ready to leave here now."

Jenny says, "Great! Candy and I are finished with our work here at the cafe. We're anxious to leave here. It's been a long busy day. We'll see you soon at the B&B."

He gathers his personal belongings and leaves for the B&B. He waves at Candy and says, "Thank You. See you later."

Aunt Jen and I wave back and say, "See you soon." We're ready to go home. Aunt Jen drove us to work in her car. We lock up the café and arrive home in about 15 minutes. That gives us enough time to change our clothes and freshen up. We ate dinner at the café during our break. The only chore we have left to do is take care of B&B business.

When Jake arrives, he's not sure if he should enter through the front door or the back. He chooses to go to the back door because he knows it leads to the kitchen. Aunt Jenny is busy in her room upstairs. I hear someone walking up the steps on the deck. I assume it's Jake especially because Lacey didn't bark. She reacts to the sound in a friendly and happy way.

When I open the back door, I see Jake looking out toward the beautiful sunset over the lake. Great timing. I love taking in the sunsets over the lake. I'm so glad I didn't miss this one. When he turns, and looks over his shoulder, I say, "Hi, Jake! Do you want to come on in?"

Lacey followed me out the door. She warms up to Jake. He reaches down and pats her on the head. They're going to be the best of friends over this weekend.

He replies, "Hi, Candy! It's really a beautiful sight to see out here. Is your Aunt Jen ready for me to sign the papers and pay for the room? I can wait out here on the deck until she's ready. I enjoy this fresh air off the water and this view is divine."

"She's upstairs. When she comes down, I'll let her know that you're waiting out here." I open the door and Lacey squeezes in ahead of me. I return to the kitchen where I make 2 cups of herbal tea. I'm anxious to sit down and relax.

Jen walks down the stairs and notices me sitting at the table with my teacup. She asks, "Did you make a cup of tea for me, too?" She smiles lovingly and with gratitude.

"Yes, Aunt Jen. I made your favorite brand just like I always do." I smile at her in return. "Jake is out on the deck waiting for you.:

"Thanks, I'll invite him in now." She opens the door and steps out on the deck. "Hi, Jake. Isn't the view of the sunset over the lake gorgeous? We can go to the kitchen now and discuss the room rental."

He replies, "Hi, Jenny. I'd like to rent the room for the weekend." They join me at the kitchen table. I offer Jake a cup of tea or coffee but he declines. I sit quietly while they finalize the room rental.

Jenny asks, "How many days and nights?"

He replies, "Let's see? Today is Thursday. How much will you charge me for tonight through Saturday night and Sunday Day? I haven't had a vacation in a long time. I feel a strong connection to nature in this beautiful house and property. I'll use these days to relax and recharge my batteries."

"I usually charge $200 to rent the room over a weekend. I'll give you a little break and say $150. Does that work for you?"

"Yes, Jenny, that works very well for me." He pulls out his checkbook and writes her a check for the full amount." All three are happy with the arrangements. Jenny asks him to fill out and sign a registration form to make it official. She reads over the form and looks up with a friendly smile. She says, "Thank you, Jacob Riley. Welcome to Happiness and the Cotton Family B&B." She gives him a key to the room and to the back door which gives him access to the kitchen.

He says, "Thank you. I'll need a few things from the car for the night. Most of my things are still packed away in my car at Al's Repair Shop."

Aunt Jen and I acknowledge what he said with a nod. While he's outside gathering his items from the car, I send a text to Darla to confirm that he'll be in the house for the weekend. Darla takes night classes at the local business college. She'll be out and about for a little longer. She often does her homework at the library on campus. Darla replies to my text with a simple, "Okay!"

Jake walks in with a small suitcase and his briefcase. He walks upstairs to his big rental room and sets his suitcase at the foot of the bed. The briefcase fits perfectly on the medium-size desk. He wants to get out of his fancy suit and relax after a long day.

He returns downstairs and asks Jenny, "Is there a schedule for the shower? I don't want to use all the hot water. Or, have a cold shower if someone else has used the hot water."

Jenny shares, "We fortunately have an industrial size hot water heater. Any time of the day should be fine. With the warmer weather, we don't worry about the pipes getting cold. Thank you for your thoughtfulness in asking. I should give you our special guest tour. Do you have time? I want you to be aware of the common area in our house. You can make yourself at home in our kitchen and in our large den/rec room. Of course, the back deck, beach and fishing pier are also available for you to enjoy."

"I would like to see the den/rec room. I saw the kitchen and my bedroom while I was here earlier today.

Jenny continues, "Also, if you need a laundromat, we have a small room for our guests that has a washer, dryer and table for folding clothes." She takes several steps toward a closed door off the kitchen. "Through that door and down the hall. You can also access it from the deck. We made it easy for our guests to use while they're enjoying the outdoors. It's a good way to take care of the wet beach towels after swimming in the lake."

"That's a good idea. I might need to take advantage of the laundromat. I have one change of casual clothes. I brought several suits on my road trip to wear at a business conference that I just attended. I was heading home when my car broke down."

I say, "That'll be fine. Maybe, tomorrow will be a convenient time for you, while Jenny and I are at the Café."

"We'll see. I need to check with Al about the status of my car tomorrow, too."

I say, "Follow me and I'll show you the den." He follows me and I ask, "Do you like relaxing by a fireplace? It's one of my favorite things to do in here."

"I don't get a chance to slow down and do things like that very often. It would be wonderful to sit in this big lovely room and escape from my problems."

I tell him, "We're out of firewood in the house. I'll have to go out to the woodpile and carry in a few logs. I'll be right back. Look around in here, make yourself at home. You're welcome as our guest to use whatever you see here. We have secure Wi-Fi and a large desk and chair. You can watch TV either here or in your room. We also have several movies available for you to watch."

He says, "I didn't notice a TV in my room. I went straight for the balcony and the beautiful view. I usually don't have time for a movie but I might want to watch a news and weather station. Please let me carry the firewood for you. Where is it?"

"The TV isn't in your room yet. We keep them stored away for safe keeping until a guest requests it. Most of our guests come here to escape their stressors and enjoy the beauty of nature. I have the impression that you want to do the same while you're here. I can set up the TV in your room, when you're ready for it."

"Okay. You're right. I want a chance to escape, rest and relax here. We can leave the TV out of my room. If you want to build a fire in the fireplace now, I'll carry the logs inside before I freshen up."

"That's a very generous offer, Jake. Thank you! Normally, I don't allow my guests to do any work around here. You seem so eager to please and I find that very refreshing. Okay, please follow me outside and I'll show you where the woodpile is located. It's outside on the other side of the house. I use a basket to carry about five logs."

After he loosens and removes his tie, he takes off his fancy suit jacket and leaves them hanging over a chair in the den. He rolls up the sleeves on his fancy white shirt. We go outside to the woodpile. I locate and place several small logs in the basket. He loads several more logs because he's strong and can carry a heavier load. After we return to the fireplace with the logs, he asks, "Do you want to make the fire or would you like for me to do the honors?"

"I'll build the fire and rest here in my favorite chair while you're upstairs. When you come down to relax, you can stir it as well as add more logs. You'll be able to relax easier by yourself. I'm ready to call it a day."

He says, "That sounds like a good plan. Thank you so much for your hospitality. I think I'll pass on the offer to enjoy the fireplace tonight. I need to take care of business on my phone and I need to reply to a few e-mails before I fall asleep tonight. I'll say good night to you then. See you in the morning?!"

"I hope your car will be okay tomorrow and that you'll enjoy your stay here. Good night!"

He says, "I'll contact Al first thing in the morning about my car. I'll see you tomorrow during the lunch hour at your awesome Café. It is fortuitous that my car broke down on the highway so close to Happiness. I believe this will be a happy weekend."

He walks upstairs to his room. I can hear him close and lock the door behind him. I also hear the water running in the shower.

I build a small fire in the fireplace. It's warm outside but the fire is comforting. I love the sound of the crackle and pop. The dancing flames are so colorful and beautiful. Watching them leap, twist and sway is almost hypnotizing. They tend to relax me too much. I sit with my feet up on the ottoman. Aunt Jen walks in and sits in a chair next to me. She wants to relax before she goes to bed. We don't talk about anything. We both understand the need for stress relief. We're hoping our B&B guest will indeed have a happy weekend.

Chapter Four

Friday Morning

Darla walks through the front door carrying her bag with books and her laptop. She calls out our names. I answer, "Darla, we're here in the den. Please join us by the fireplace."

When she walks into the den, she's smiling at us and her eyes are twinkling. She's happy and excited to share her good news. "I made the Dean's List. I'm very happy that my hard work is paying off. I believe it'll look good on my resume."

I say, "Congratulations! We should celebrate this weekend. I'm so very happy for you. I remember the joy I felt the first time I made the Dean's List. You've been working long hard hours both in school and here at the house. Keep up the good work, Darla."

Aunt Jen says, "Congratulations, Darla! I know your parents will be proud. I really appreciate the hard work that you do for us. We'll figure out a special way to celebrate your achievement.

Darla says, "Thank you, Aunt Jen and Candy. I'm going up to my room now. I'm exhausted. I want to get ready for bed."

I tell her, "I sent you a text today but I want to remind you that Jake is our B&B guest. He'll be staying with us tonight through Sunday. Do you remember the nice man from this afternoon? He's staying in the same room that you showed him today."

"Okay, thanks for the reminder. It slipped my mind because of the college classes. Good night to both of you. I'll see you bright and early in the morning.

When Darla reaches the top of the stairs, Jake opens the door to his room. They both nod and say, "Good Night!" She continues to walk down the hall to her room and closes her door for the night. He continues his walk down the stairs and to the den.

"Hello, Candy and Jenny. That's a lovely fire. I hope you two enjoyed it. I've had a long and stressful day. Maybe, tomorrow night I can have the pleasure. I'm exhausted. What time do you serve breakfast in the morning? I'll set my alarm."

I reply, "Tomorrow night will be a fine night for us to build another fire. Darla wakes up at 7:00am to bake fresh rolls. Our breakfast is like a continental breakfast. She usually has everything setup and ready to eat by 8:00am. By the way, there is a waffle house in town if you prefer a bigger breakfast while you're in town. We don't serve breakfast at our café because we don't want to be in competition with our good friends."

Jake says, "Maybe, Sunday morning will be a good day to check out the waffle house. Thanks! Your breakfast menu will work just fine for me in the morning.

Jake sets an alarm for 8:00am and goes to work on his cell phone and e-mail messages. He only replies to the ones marked high priority and personal messages from his family. He's able to sleep peacefully for the first time in years. The house and area are quiet. His stress level is not as high and he feels an increase level of joy.

Aunt Jen and I know that Friday through the weekend are the busiest days for us at the café. We're hoping for a peaceful restful sleep tonight.

I take Lacey out for a quick walk before going to bed. It's a beautiful moonlit night. On my way, back to the house I see Jake standing out on his balcony looking out at the lake. He's a very handsome man and even more so in the moonlight. He waves but doesn't say anything.

When Jake notices Candy walking Lacey in the moonlight he thinks, *"Candy is really a beautiful young lady. She's breathtaking, especially in the moonlight."*

They're all sleeping soundly now. Lacey is snoring and curled up on her bed at the foot of my bed.

Darla wakes up to her alarm at 7:00am. She dresses in a suitable outfit for cooking in the kitchen. She preheats the oven while she prepares the coffee and tea. The aroma of the fresh brewed coffee and rolls is a wonderful way to wake up. She prepares this breakfast for their B&B guest and for the 3 family members living in this house.

She sets out the jelly and jams as well as a bowl of fresh fruit. Orange juice is also available. Coffee creamer and sugar are placed by the coffee and tea dispensers. Plates, napkins, silverware, mugs are set up buffet style. The rolls are hot and ready to eat.

Aunt Jen and I are used to this routine every morning. Today we'll leave for work between 10:30am and 11:00am. We open the café doors at noon for the lunch crowd. My first stop in the kitchen is at the coffee pot. I fill a mug of coffee for Aunt Jen, Darla and myself. There's no sign that our guest is awake.

When Aunt Jen enters the kitchen, I help Darla serve our breakfast meals at the table. We usually try to eat while the rolls are hot. As a rule, we try to give our guests the freedom to enjoy their breakfast in solitude.

Jake appears before they are finished. He walks in and says, "The coffee and rolls smell delicious. Is it okay if I join you at the table? How are you ladies doing this morning"

I say, "Good morning, Jake. I'm doing very well, thank you. How are you doing this morning? Did you sleep well? It's okay with me for you to join us here. I'm almost finished here. I would like a coffee refill but I can drink it in the den or out on the deck."

Aunt Jen replies, "I'm doing very well, too. Thanks for asking. Yes, it's okay with me, too. Please help yourself to whatever you would like to eat or drink here. Just let us know if you can't find what you need, we'll be happy to help."

Darla says, "Good Morning. I'm doing very well and I hope you're doing well, too."

Jake says, "I slept very well. I woke up feeling very refreshed. Candy, please don't leave on my account. Eating a meal sitting out on the deck is tempting. Perhaps, I'll enjoy a second cup of coffee out there later. Is it okay if I sit down at the head of the table? Because I'm so tall, that spot at a table usually gives me enough room to feel comfortable.?

Darla says, "That's fine, Jake."

While he fills his plate, I automatically place a knife, fork and spoon on a napkin for him at the end of the table. He sits down after pouring coffee in a mug.

Darla asks, "Aunt Jen and Candy, are we going to take a walk around the lake this morning? It looks like it's going to be another beautiful sunny day."

I reply, "Yes, I was just wondering about that myself. We better hurry before we run out of time. I'll put the leash and harness on Lacey."

Aunt Jen replies, "Oh, yes! I believe it'll be a beautiful day, too. I'm ready to go when you are."

I ask, "Jake, are you interested in a walk around the lake with us this morning? No pressure intended. You can relax and enjoy your meal in solitude."

Jake says, "I would love to join all of you for a walk. Can you please wait for about five more minutes? I would like to find my camera and a pair of sneakers."

I reply, "Yes, I think we can wait for you. I'm going to get Lacey ready to go and we'll wait for you on the deck."

Darla clears the table and stores the cold food items in the refrigerator. She returns all the breakfast items to their proper place. Aunt Jen washes the dishes and leaves them on a drain board to air dry. They always work hard and fast because they've learned not to waste precious time.

When Jake is finished eating, he goes up to his room to find his camera and a pair of sneakers. When he returns to the kitchen, he realizes that we're waiting patiently for him on the deck. As soon as Jake is out the door, we begin our walk around the lake. Lacey's tail is whipping around and she's running in circles. She's so excited to be out on this beautiful day. Jake enjoys everything about this new adventure. Lacey's happy and playful mood lifts his spirits.

While Jake chats and laughs with us, he hears the ringtone on his cell phone. He checks it. The ID reads, 'Al's Auto Repair Shop'. He says, 'I've got to take this call. It's about my car. Please excuse me. Please continue without me. I don't want to cause a delay that will make you late for work. See you later."

He answers the call and continues his walk back to the house. He answers with anticipation, "Good morning, Al. How are you today?"

"Hello, Jacob. Good morning to you, too. I have bad news. I won't be able to complete the repairs on your car, today. I need a part that I do not have in stock. The auto parts store says they can deliver it to me tomorrow. I'm sorry for any inconvenience."

Jakes says, "I'm definitely disappointed. As it turns out, I'm staying the weekend at the Cotton Family B&B. I'm not planning to leave until Sunday afternoon. It should work out okay. I'm anxious to have my car fixed. Thanks for calling and letting me know."

Al says, "Thank you for understanding. We really appreciate our customers. Enjoy your weekend. The B&B is really a beautiful place. The family is loving and kind."

"I agree. Their hospitality is greatly appreciated. I hope to see you and pick up my car tomorrow. See you later."

Al says, "Goodbye. See you later."

Jake arrives back at the house and enters the kitchen. He pours a second mug of coffee and takes it down to a table close to the beach. He sees us walking on the other side of the lake. He takes a few sips of the coffee before he decides to jog toward us. Jogging is good exercise in this fresh air. It'll be fun for all of us to visit again while we make our return trip home. Besides that, Jake is growing fond of Lacey and her energetic outlook on life.

He returns the empty mug to the kitchen sink before he starts jogging. The clear level path makes it easy to catch up with them. Lacey's energy is renewed when she sees Jake. She starts barking playfully and tugs on the leash. I decide to let go of the leash for this short distance. I know that she wants to play with Jake. It's amazing how she's taken to him in a short time. They act as though they've known each other a lifetime.

When we arrive home, we're serious about going our separate ways to get ready for the day ahead. It's almost time for Aunt Jen and me to leave for the café. Darla has her work cut out for her, too.

I ask, "Jake? Did Al fix your car for you? Is everything working out for you?"

He replies, "No. Al says it needs a part that cannot be delivered until tomorrow. I'm happy that staying at your B&B worked out for me." I think I'll take my camera outside and take a few more pictures of this area. I would like to take a few pictures in town, too. Is it okay if I take a few inside your café and the B&B part of your house?"

Aunt Jen says, "Yes, that's fine."

He replies, "That'll give me something to do before eating lunch at your café. I'm disappointed about my car. It'll be good to keep busy and not worry over it."

Chapter Five

Jake Lends a Hand

In keeping with my usual routine, I take Lacey for a walk before leaving for the café for the day. Darla takes care of her needs while I'm away. Jake is walking around the front and back yards with his high-tech camera. I'm not sure why Lacey is so taken with him. Lacey takes off and runs toward him looking for his attention.

I call out, "Lacey! Laaacey!" I let out a little whistle and continue to call her, "Come here, Lacey. Come here, girl. Time to go inside."

I catch up with her, while Jake is down on one knee patting her head and scratching her head behind her ears. That's the attention she wanted from him. Lacey's wagging tail gives away the fact she's happy and likes Jake.

Jake says, "I'm finished taking pictures of the beautiful scenery outside. It looks like today will be another beautiful day here in Happiness. I captured several great shots of the lake and trees. Is it okay if I take a picture of you and Lacey with the lake in the background?"

"Hm? Why do you want our picture?"

Jake replies, "I'm going to create a photo album to share my weekend adventure with my family back home. I'm having a wonderful time here. These are memorable moments that I want to last a lifetime. Is it okay? If you don't like the picture, I will delete it."

I reply, "None of our guests have ever asked me to pose for their photo shoots. I guess it'll be okay. I know Aunt Jen gave you permission to take pictures of the B&B and outside area. I appreciate the fact that you asked me first before candidly snapping a picture of me. I doubt that Lacey will mind if you want to include her in your photo shoot. I really need to take Lacey inside because it's time for Aunt Jen and me to leave for work."

"Smile? You are beautiful and I think you are photogenic. Will you please take a second to pose for me? I may not get another chance to capture a shot like this again. I can stay out here and play with Lacey for a few minutes. I don't have anything else planned until the lunch hour."

"Okay, how's this?" I ask Lacey to sit and I get down on one knee with my hand on her back.

He takes the picture and says, "That's really great. It's a winner! Thank you, Candy and Lacey. I won't keep you any longer. I hope you have a happy day."

"If you want to follow me, I'll show you where Lacey's outdoor toys are stored." He follows me to the deck and I show him the plastic crate under the deck. It holds Lacey's Frisbee, a couple of plastic hard bones and several different sizes of balls to play catch. One is an old tennis ball which I think is her favorite. If you want to play with Lacey, I'm sure she would love for you to toss the tennis ball around for her to chase. It's been awhile since I've had time to play a game of Frisbee with her. She might enjoy catching the Frisbee with you, too. Thank you for your kindness."

"It's my pleasure. I haven't taken time to play with a dog for several years. My job keeps me too busy to have time for fun things like this. It will be good exercise for both of us."

I say, "I have to leave now. I'll see you later." I take time to wash my hands before catching up with Aunt Jen who is already out the door and heading to the car. We can't afford to be late.

Jake fishes the tennis ball out the crate and sees that Lacey is interested in playing. He leads her around to the side of the house where they first met. He tosses the ball and Lacey chases it and returns it by dropping it at his feet. They play like this until Lacey shows signs of being tired and a bit overheated. He takes her into the house so that she can get a drink from her water bowl. Darla is running a vacuum cleaner so she doesn't hear Jake come in the back door.

He's thirsty and peeks in the refrigerator to determine his options. Darla hears him in the kitchen. She walks over and stands beside him. Her sudden presence startles him.

In a professional but friendly tone, she asks, "How can I help you?"

He responds, "I'm looking for a cold drink. I feel a little overheated after playing with Lacey outside. Do you have sweet tea? If not, what do you have that I can drink to feel refreshed again?"

"Yes, we have sweet tea? Do you want it on ice?"

He answers, "Yes, I can get the tea for myself. I don't want to inconvenience you. I heard that you were busy running the vacuum cleaner."

"I'm finished with the vacuum cleaner for now. I'll run it again when it does not disturb you. I can serve you. It's my job to take care of our guests."

He asks, "Will you please serve it in one of your to-go paper cups? I want to sit out on the deck. After that, I'll go for a walk down to the beach and the fishing pier?"

"That is a good idea." She finds a large plastic cup with a lid and straw. She asks, "Will this to-go cup work for your outdoor adventures?"

He nods and says, "Thank you. It's perfect." Looking around the room, he sees that Lacey is stretched on the floor resting. While walking over to the back door, Lacey doesn't move from her resting place. Jake proceeds to sit on a lounge chair on the deck in a shaded area. It's been awhile since he checked his phone for messages. He thinks about doing it but decides to wait until he's inside without the glare.

After resting and drinking the iced sweet tea, he pitches the cup into a trash can. He starts walking down to the beach and the fishing pier when Darla appears on the deck. She calls out to him, "Sir? Jake? If you want to go fishing or row a boat out on the lake, I can show you where our boat and fishing poles are stored. I know that you're stuck here because your car is at Al's repair shop. There's not a lot to do around here."

"Thank you, Darla, that sounds like fun. I haven't been fishing or out in a boat for a long time. Maybe after I return here from the café this afternoon. I'm planning to leave here soon and eat lunch." He checks the time on his wristwatch and adds, "I'll just take a walk out to the pier for now. I want a few minutes to connect with the beauty of nature for now."

She says with a smile, "That is what most of our guests like to do the most here." They find happiness in the beauty and breathing fresh air. Have a good day!"

He stands at the end of the pier with both hands on the rails looking out over the lake and breathing in as much air as his lungs can hold. Slowly, he exhales as though he's trying to release a ton of tension from his physical body. His emotions are pent up and his mind is on stress overload. He needed this escape more than he realized before. He's beginning to have a clearer outlook on life. He feels like a ton of bricks has been lifted off his shoulders.

With a new bounce in his step, he walks back to the house and up the stairs to his room. He freshens up and dresses in a clean suit. His only casual outfit is no longer fresh due to his time playing with Lacey outside. After double checking his pockets for the car and B&B keys, he finds Darla downstairs. He asks, "Would you like a sandwich from the deli at the café? Or, maybe a treat from the bakery?"

Her eyes widen and she flashes a broad smile. She replies, "Oh, Sir. You are very kind to offer to do that for me. I like their club sandwiches. Are you sure that's not an inconvenience? I need to find my purse upstairs and give you the cash to pay for it. I'll be right back."

"It's okay, Darla. I can cover this. It's a chance for me to return the kindness you have shown me. It's not an inconvenience at all. What about the bakery? Is there a pastry or pie that you would like from the café? I ate a piece of apple pie yesterday that was delicious."

"I love the apple pie from the bakery at the café. It's always fresh baked. Please don't go to any trouble. I'm very grateful to have the club sandwich. I often work hard here and forget to take time to eat a lunch meal."

"I thought about buying a whole pie yesterday. I'll buy a whole pie today and we can all share it over this weekend. Talking about apple pie is making me hungry. I'll leave for the café now. See you later. Have a good afternoon."

When he arrives at the Candy Cotton Café in town, there's not a place to park the car. He locates a spot two blocks away. The crowd is bigger on Friday than it was yesterday. He observes the license plates are from several different counties in the surrounding area. People drive several miles to enjoy the food served at the café.

This time when the bell jingles on the door, he's not surprised. No one looks over to check him out. He no longer feels like a stranger trying to fit in. He waits in line and places his order for today's special. It's a foot-long sub with the works which is a man size sandwich. He'll order Darla's club sandwich before he leaves the café. It'll be fresher for her that way.

A table isn't available but there's an empty bar stool. He chooses to sit there while he eats his sandwich and drinks the refreshing sweet tea. He looks around for Candy but doesn't see her. When he's finished eating, he stands in line again to order Darla's sandwich and an apple pie to go.

Jenny walks by and says, "Hello, Jake. Glad to see you made it here for lunch. How was your sandwich?"

"Good afternoon, Jenny. My sandwich was delicious. Thank you for asking. Where's Candy? Is she doing okay? With the size of this crowd, I expected to see her busy out here."

Jenny replies, "Oh, she's busy in the kitchen. Our dishwasher didn't show up due to an injury. We're taking turns filling in. I'm bussing the tables while she rinses the dishes and loads them in our industrial size dishwasher."

"My first job as a teenager was a dishwasher at a big fancy restaurant. I've got a little experience and a lot of extra time on my hands. Would you like some help? I'll be happy to volunteer."

Jenny reacts, "Are you sure you want to do that? I can pay you temp wages. Candy and I both appreciate a helping hand. We'll be happy to have your help. You're very strong and you always seem eager to please. Thank you, Jake. The lunch crowd should thin out in about an hour."

"I don't need the money. No need to pay me anything. Show me where to find the kitchen sink and I'll relieve Candy from her shift."

Jenny says, "Do you have a baseball cap? We'll need to find a way to cover your hair."

Yes, in the car but I'm parked two blocks away. It'll take a few minutes to retrieve it and change my shoes from dress to sneakers. I'll be right back"

He hurries down the sidewalk like a man on a mission. When he gets to his car, he removes his tie, suit jacket, and dress shoes. He rolls up his sleeves and puts on his sneakers. He's grateful that he chose to wear one of his less expensive suits. At last, he places his baseball cap squarely on his head. He hurries back to the café. The crowd is a lot quieter now.

He checks in with Jenny and she leads him to the kitchen sink where I'm rinsing dishes. Aunt Jen finds a clean white apron and hands it to him. He puts it on with a smile as though he's recalling a happy memory. I say, "Thank you, Jake, for your generous offer to lend us a helping hand."

Chapter Six
No Paparazzi Please

Jake explains to Jenny and me, "I've always felt ambitious and I like to keep busy. I also like to help when I see people in need of a helping hand. The timing was right for all of us. I was in the right place at the right time. I noticed you ladies don't waste your time. You work hard and get the job done. I'm like that to a fault. I'm a workaholic. Now, that I've had a chance to slow down this weekend, I'll need to make a few changes in my life. I need to take time to breathe and enjoy doing fun things like I used to in my younger days."

I say, "We appreciate meeting you and your generous help here today. Running the sprayer and the dishwasher are easy to do but very time consuming. We've had a lot of customers eat in at our café."

"I'll be happy to keep working at it until the job is done. Please don't let me forget to buy a club sandwich and an apple pie to go. I'm buying the sandwich for Darla and the apple pie for all of us to share."

"You're very generous to do that. I won't let you forget. In fact, I'll let you have those two items free of charge as a way of saying thank you. It's not necessary to clean all the dishes. We just need help in catching up on the workload. The work will be finished a lot faster with three people. I need to go out front and take care of customers. If you need anything or have a question, please let me know."

Jake is a success in helping them catch up. The lunch rush has passed. He removes the apron. He's ready for a break and a tall glass of iced sweet tea. After the break, he orders Darla's sandwich and a whole apple pie to go.

I fill his to-go-order and give him the tea, sandwich and pie for free. He says, "Thank you! I'm going to take Darla's sandwich to the B&B so that she can eat it while it's still fresh. She might think that I've forgotten her by this time. I'll place the pie in your refrigerator. Please help yourself and enjoy." He waves goodbye with a big smile. "I'll see you later."

Darla is thrilled to eat her favorite sandwich out on the deck. Jake makes room for the pie on a shelf in the refrigerator. He goes upstairs to refresh and changes into another suit. It's either time to go shopping or time to do the laundry. It doesn't take long for him to realize that he needs to do both. After he carries his laundry bag downstairs, he puts his old casual clothes in the washing machine first. He'll return to finish the rest of the laundry, later.

He walks out on the deck and asks Darla, "Can you give me directions to a men's clothing store?"

She replies, "Yes, I have a brochure with a map that will help you find your way." She goes to a stand in the den and pulls out the brochure. While handing it to him, she says, "This men's store sells both casual and dress clothing for men."

He takes the brochure and his camera for a trip downtown. This will be a good time for a photo shoot. He'll take pictures of the town of Happiness for his weekend adventure album. After locating the men's store, he buys several casual pants and shirts as well as a new pair of casual shoes. He takes at least a dozen pics of things and places in the downtown area. When he recalls that his laundry needs his attention, he wastes no time driving back to the B&B.

When he arrives, he notices a new car parked out front. He assumes it's another guest checking in. While walking up the steps of the deck, he sees a beautiful young lady talking to Darla. Because he doesn't want to intrude, he walks by without saying a word. He goes straight to the laundry room and places the first load into the dryer. After clipping the tags off his new clothes, he puts the new pants in the washer for his second load. He decides to wash the new shirts separately.

He helps himself to a glass of iced sweet tea in the kitchen. He uses a to-go cup with the plan to take it outside and relax on the beach. He sets a timer on his watch so that he can finish the laundry in due time. Lacey is following him around like she wants more attention. Although, he's not up to playing with her, he finds her harness and leash to take her for a short walk. Because Darla is talking and busy, he assumes it will be okay to walk Lacey and give her a little attention.

Darla is talking with Denise because she's an overnight guest at the B&B. Denise carries a suitcase and briefcase in from her car. After a quick guided tour, she receives a key to her room and the back door.

After Jake walks Lacey, he checks on his laundry. He folds his clean clothes and proceeds to carry them upstairs to his room. He passes Darla and Denise in the hallway. Darla introduces Jake to her.

Jake says, "Hello, Denise, I'm delighted to meet you."

She stares into Jake's eyes. There's a moment of recognition and her jaw drops. She stammers and stutters because she is star struck. She says, "Aren't you? Are YOU Jacob…"

He replies, "Please, Denise, I'd like to remain low-key. If you think you know me, please let me stay anonymous to these fine people here in Happiness."

"Yes, I've seen your picture in the money magazines and newspaper articles. Okay, I promise not to reveal your identity. I value my privacy and will respect yours. I'm delighted to meet you."

"Please, excuse me, Ma'am, I need to go to my room and put this laundry away. Thank you for respecting my wishes. I hope you enjoy your stay here. I've enjoyed my experience at the Cotton Family B&B."

Denise says, "I'm sure I will. This is not my first time as a guest here. Candy and I are old acquaintances. She and I went to the same high school and we attended a few college classes together. We're long-time friends. Maybe we'll meet again during this weekend."

Jake goes into his room and locks the door. While taking care of the laundry, he realizes the need for a new travel bag. There's not enough room in his suitcase for his new clothes. Although he needs a break before supper, he wants to check his messages. He slips off his shoes and stretches out on the bed and props up using the pillows against the headboard.

He's had a full day of activity already and wonders what is next? He reads the texts and e-mail on his cell phone. After replying to a couple of texts from family members and one from his workplace, he saves the rest for later.

He sets a timer to rest and relax for about 10 minutes. When the timer chimes, he stretches and yawns. Feeling hungry for supper prompts him to get up and get ready for the trip to Candy Cotton Café. After he's ready to go, he steps out on the balcony to take in the view and breathe the fresh air. He inhales and exhales ever so slowly.

While opening his door, he listens for voices or movement in the house and B&B. No one is around except for Lacey. She's perfectly content laying on her bed. He thinks maybe Darla left for her night classes at the college. He walks out on the patio and once again breathes the fresh air. When he arrives at the café, the crowd on a Friday night is full of life, vim and vigor.

He decides to go shopping for a new travel bag while waiting for the crowd in the cafe to thin out. Denise is also shopping in the same department store. They see each other on the escalator. It's laughable to them that she's riding down while he's riding up the escalator. They smile at each other and wave hello.

After Jake purchases a new bag, he drives back to the café. The crowd has thinned considerably. While sitting in a different spot in the café, he sees a small TV up over the coffee bar. He didn't notice it today when he was there for lunch. But now he sees his picture on the screen. It seems the paparazzi have been looking for him. They think he's disappeared off the face of the earth. He laughs out loud at the news report.

He thinks, *I guess I'll need a disguise if word gets out that I'm alive and well in the small town of Happiness. So far, I've managed to keep my business identity under wraps. I would like to keep it that way at least through Sunday.*

The waitress walks over and takes his order. She returns with a glass of water as he requested. He looks around for Candy and Jenny once again but he doesn't see them. He asks the waitress and she tells him Candy is washing dishes. Jenny is taking care of business in their office.

He asks the waitress, "Will you please tell Candy that I'm here for a supper meal? Please tell her, too, that I'll be happy to help her again if needed."

The waitress asks, "What is your name?"

He replies, "Tell her, Jake."

The waitress serves his meal in short order. He's half way through it when I appear in front of his table. I say, "HI, Jake! How are you tonight? The waitress told me you were here and offering to clean dishes for us again. Is that true?"

"It's true. I'm willing to wash a few more dishes for you. Do you need my assistance here tonight?"

I say, "That will be great but please finish eating your meal first. Aunt Jenny and I haven't had a dinner break, yet. We want to eat as soon as we're caught up on the dinner rush. Whenever you're ready to help, please come on back. You know where to find me. I'll pay for your meal to say thank you for your help again."

"That's not necessary for you to pay for my meal. I've got the money. It's my pleasure to help a hard-working lady. I'll be there as soon as I'm finished with my meal."

He pays the waitress for the meal and gives her a generous tip. After going back to the car for his cap and tennis shoes, he takes over the job of cleaning the dishes.

I say, "Thank you, once again, Jake." I rush off to finish the work in the dining area.

While he's busy rinsing the dishes and silverware, he hears the office door open down the hall. He recognizes Jenny's voice but not the person who is giggling. Denise appears in the doorway of the kitchen with a surprised look on her face.

She says, "Well, hello, Jacob. We do meet again. I bet the paparazzi would have a field day if they could see you now."

Jake says, "Shh! Please, Denise. Please let me enjoy my time here in the café and the B&B. I won't be staying in Happiness much longer. I'm only here because I had car trouble on the highway. This is where the tow truck brought my car to be repaired. I'm leaving here to return home on Sunday. Please just let me have this time without giving away my identity."

"Okay. I promise. It's shocking to see you dressed in a fancy business shirt and dress pants while you're washing the dishes. I apologize. I didn't mean to cause you any grief. Candy would not be happy with me for harassing one of her guests. I'm truly sorry."

Jake says, "Thank you, Denise. Anonymity is important to me. I've enjoyed my adventure here a lot and I look forward to visiting here again without the paparazzi chasing me."

Chapter Seven
Jake Needs a Break

Jake rinses and loads the last plate in the dishwasher. Now, he's ready for a break. The second shift had more dishes, pots, pans and utensils to clean than the first. Volunteering to help at the cafe gives him happy feelings but physically it's exhausting.

After removing his apron and cap, he walks down the hall to the office. He tells Jenny, "I'm caught up on cleaning in the kitchen. I'm really exhausted. Without a doubt, I need to go back to the B&B to rest and relax. My back is feeling sore. See you later."

Jenny says, "Thank you very much Jake. We appreciate your kindness and generosity in helping us in a pinch. I'll see you later tonight. I do hope you can relax and feel better soon."

"I'll tell Candy goodbye on my way out." He smiles.

Jake walks up to me while I'm working in the dining room. He looks totally drained. I offer him a cold beverage. He says, "Thank you. I'm planning to go to the B&B to rest. Maybe on the beach under a shade tree." He laughs. "Sounds like a good plan. I'm sure the sunset will be beautiful over the lake."

I say, "Oh, yes, sounds like a wonderful plan. I'll want to do that on Sunday, which is my day off. Or, on Monday, we're closed here at the café. How about a glass of iced tea to-go? My treat of course to say thank you for rescuing me, again."

"I think I'll take a seat at my favorite table and rest while I drink the tea. I need a chance to catch my breath before driving home." He sits down while I pour the tea into a glass filled with ice. I serve the glass of sweet tea on a coaster.

He smiles and says, "Thank you, Candy!"

I cheerfully say, "You're welcome for the tea. I know how hard you worked."

"Do you have time to join me at the table with a glass of tea, too?"

I reply, "Sure. I just need to take care of one thing behind the counter. After that, I'll bring a glass of tea over and we can visit for a few minutes."

I complete my work behind the counter. I'm grateful for a chance to take a break with Jake. After pouring a glass of iced tea for myself, I sit down with Jake at the table. He's looking more energized. The tea is very refreshing for both of us.

Jake asks, "Do you mind if I ask you a few personal questions?"

I respond, "What about? Is there a problem that I can help with?"

"I don't want to impose on you or your friends. I would like to know more about Denise. Because she's staying at the B&B this weekend, I'm curious about her outgoing personality. She said you two were old classmates. I met her earlier at the B&B and here at the café. We had an encounter that's causing me concern. I hope that I'm not being too forward or impolite. It's a security issue from my perspective."

I ask, "Do you want to tell me what's going on? If there's a problem, I would want to help. You've been a perfect gentleman and very generous with your time. I remember how outgoing Denise used to be in school and college. She was always flirting and talking big. Her outgoing personality has served her well. Denise has made a name for herself as a high-powered career woman. We like to get together when she returns to town. That's why she's renting a room at the B&B. She was passing through this area on a business trip. We like to share a meal, spend time out by the lake, just do fun things together and catch up on what's new in our lives."

"I'm enjoying my stay at your B&B and I look forward to the weekend there. Without giving away too much information, I want to spend my time here very low-key. When Darla introduced us, Denise recognized me and knows my identity. I asked her not to say anything to anyone because I want to enjoy my time here without any confusion. I certainly don't want to bring any trouble to you or your family. If she reveals my identity, I'm afraid her actions could cause a frenzy of reporters on your doorstep."

"I don't know who you are but I completely understand your need for an escape here in Happiness. I respect your desire to just rest and relax without added stress. That is one of the reasons my family decided to renovate and open part of our large house. We love the house, the yard with the large trees, the lake, etc. We realize there's a need for people to get away from their routines and problems. A chance to breathe and feel relieved from stress that affects our health. What can I do to help?"

Jake says, "I'm not sure that you can DO anything. I just felt the need to talk to someone about my concerns. Is Denise the type of person that would give away my identity? If she is, I may have to leave here. I need to protect my family, too."

"I can talk to her but just sitting here right now, I'd say she's honest and respectful. If you asked her not to say anything, I believe that she'll honor your request. I'll be meeting with her later. If you want, I can talk to her about this. I certainly want you to find peace and enjoy your time here."

Jake shares, "Thank you, but I don't think it's necessary for you to talk to Denise for me. I do appreciate you taking time to listen. Ever since my encounter with her today, I've felt queasy and uptight. I'm concerned for my family back home. I keep thinking how much my family would enjoy being here with me right now. But I can't take a chance on things being blown out of proportion in the media. I want all of us to be safe and happy. I wish I could share more with you but it just doesn't seem the right time or place."

I say, "It's okay, Jake. I do hope you're feeling better now. I appreciate meeting you and your kindness. I'm happy to support your need for rest and relaxation at our B&B this weekend. The time is getting late, I need to finish up and lockup here. Are you feeling well enough to drive now?"

"Yes, I'm feeling much better. I'll feel even better when I'm sitting on the beach at the B&B. I've thought about the joy of doing that all day. I long for the chance to breathe in the fresh air and let go of all the stress of the day. Have fun with your friend. I'm relieved that you believe we'll have peace under the same roof. I'll see you later."

I cheerfully say, "I'll see you later. We'll be back home in time to enjoy the fireplace before bed, tonight."

I'm on my way to meet up with Denise. I'm glad Jake trusted me enough to share his concerns. I want our guests at the B&B to feel safe and secure.

Whatever reason Jake wants privacy, I believe he's a good man and cares about his family. I respect him a lot for that. I also care about my family and want them to feel safe.

When Jake arrives at the B&B, first thing on his agenda is rest and relaxation. He goes to his room to change and freshen up. An old casual outfit is perfect for the beach today. It's been a long time since he took time off from work to have fun in the sun. Before he puts on his old pants, he takes a pair of scissors and cuts the pant legs just above the knee. The last time he wore cut-off pants was in college at a beach party with his buddies.

While passing through the kitchen, he spots Lacey and tells her hello. She's half asleep but wags her tail to acknowledge his attention. He pats her on the head lovingly. He opens the refrigerator looking for a cold beverage. He takes a cup of sweet tea out with him to the beach and sits down on a lounge chair. He inhales and exhales slowly trying to release the tension in his body. Taking in the beauty of nature in front of him, he lets go and totally relaxes.

He's just about to doze off when he feels a light sprinkle of water teasing him. Out of the blue, it seems mother nature wants a rain shower. It was short and sweet as well as refreshing. In fact, the rainbow over the lake adds to the beauty. He's never felt relaxed like this before and feels very grateful.

This is a great time to take pictures for his new album. He goes up to his room for the camera. He returns to the beach and captures several memorable nature shots. The beautiful rainbow took center stage.

He hears Lacey barking at the back door. While going in to investigate, Darla is struggling with Lacey trying to put her leash on. Lacey is reacting with high energy because she's excited to see Jake. He asks, "Would you like me to take her out for a walk? I am considering walking around the lake."

Darla responds with a big smile, "Yes, of course. That would be helpful and I'm sure Lacey will love it."

While walking with Lacey on the path around the lake, the phone rings. Jake answers and hears a child's voice say, "Hello, Daddy?"

"Hello, Son, yes, this is your Daddy. How are you, David? How was school today? I'm so glad you called me. I wish you were here with me."

David answers, "I miss you, Dad. I thought you were going to be home today. After school, I looked for you in every room of our house. Where are you? When will you be home? Nanny and I are sad because we missed you all week."

His Daddy explains, "My car broke down on the highway while I was driving home yesterday. The tow truck driver delivered my car to a mechanic in the closest town. The name of the town is Happiness. Isn't that a neat name? Al, the mechanic said that he'll try to fix it tomorrow. Didn't Nanny tell you about this?"

"Yes, Nanny told me about your car yesterday and she said you would be home on Sunday. "I miss you very much, Daddy. I wish that we could be together this whole weekend."

"I wish we could be together too but I'm too far away to drive there in Al's loaner car. I'll be home as soon as I can on Sunday. I can't wait to see you"

Lacey is romping around making it difficult for Jake to hold onto the leash and talk on the phone at the same time. Jake explains to his Son, "I'll call you back in a few minutes. I'm walking a dog and she's pulling hard on the leash. I almost dropped my phone."

David responds with excitement, "A Dog? What kind of dog? Will you send me a pic on Nanny's cell phone?"

"Ask Nanny really quick if it's okay." David turns and asks the Nanny if it's okay. She nods in agreement. "She said it's okay, Dad."

"I'll send you a selfie of Lacey and me. I really need to go for now. I'll talk to you soon, I promise. Be on your best behavior for Nanny, okay? Bye, Son."

"Bye, Dad. I'll be waiting for you to call me."

Jake gently commands Lacey to sit. He gets down on one knee and takes a selfie of them together to send to his son. He manages to capture the beauty of the sunset in the background. While sharing the selfie in a text to Nanny, he has a happy thought which comes like a flash of light. He needs to find Jenny and ask if the idea will work out or not. He hurries back to the B&B.

Aunt Jen and I are relaxing and chatting on the back deck. Jake walks up the steps with a big grin and says, "Can I talk to you in a few minutes? I need to ask you an important question. I'll take Lacey in and then I'll check back with you in a minute."

Both Aunt Jen and I say, "Okay."

He takes Lacey inside and unhooks the leash from her collar. Lacey heads straight for her water dish. He takes a deep breath and thinks twice about what he must say. He hopes they will respond favorably. He steps out on the deck, "Is this a good time for me to ask my question? I don't want to spoil your time together. The sunset is gorgeous. I'm happy that you two didn't miss it."

Jenny says. "Yes, this is a perfect time. Please sit down and relax with us."

Chapter Eight
I Miss You, Daddy

I ask them, "Do you want me to leave?"

Jake tells me, "No. I'd like for you to hear my question, too, Candy." He pauses and inhales deeply while he shares, "First, I need to say, I have an idea that I'd like to see become reality with your help. Can we keep our conversation confidential? Is that okay?"

I say, "Yes, I respect your need for privacy." Aunt Jen follows my lead and reassures him to speak freely.

"My son, David, called me today while I was out on a walk with Lacey. He's eight years old. We miss each other a lot. Today, after school, he searched for me through the whole house because he thought I would be home from my business trip. If it hadn't been for the car trouble, I'd be sitting at home with him right now. My big question is, do you take in families with children in your B&B? I would like to figure out a way for David to be with me here in this lovely town of Happiness. Would it be okay for me to set up a cot in my room for him? He's small and won't take up much room."

I'm totally taken aback as I did not realize Jake had a young son. Aunt Jen takes it all in stride and says, "Yes, we can add a cot to your room or the loveseat in your room pulls out and makes a comfy bed."

"Thank you for understanding. I'm grateful for your support and positive feedback." He takes out his wallet and shows us a picture of David. He's a very cute freckle-faced eight-year-old boy and he's smiling up at his dad. The picture looks like it was taken at a birthday party.

He continues to share his story. "Before the car problems, I was anxious to be home with my son for the weekend. We have a Nanny that cares for him throughout the week. Our original plan was for her to spend this weekend with her family. Anyway, If I can discreetly bring him here, we can have fun playing at the beach. Darla said you have a small boat and fishing poles. It would be a dream come true for David and me to share an experience like I had with my Grandpa."

I ask, "Is it okay if I ask you a question?"

"Sure, if you're willing to keep the answer confidential."

"What do you mean by discreetly?"

Do you remember when we spoke earlier about Denise and my concern that she would reveal my identity? When I travel, I drive my own car and try to disguise myself to avoid unwanted attention. I noticed on a news report that the reporters are looking for me. They think that I've dropped off the face of the earth. I want my son to make the trip here without reporters stalking us. I can think of several options but can't decide which is best. Now that I have your approval, I'll call David and make arrangements with our Nanny."

I cheerfully say, "I hope that you're able to work out the fine details to your satisfaction. If we can do anything at all to help you bring your son out here, we'll happily do it. We'll be happy to see you two together here at our B&B. Having a young child here, will be a pleasure."

"Thank you, I'm going to my room to make the call. I hope to see you both later. I'm looking forward to a fireside chat tonight." He leaves with a warm friendly smile. After he closes the door to his room, he stretches out on the bed. He calls Nanny on her cell phone.

She answers, "Good evening, Jake. David is anxious to talk to you. I'm glad you were able to call him back tonight."

He urgently tells her, "I'd like to speak with you first, please. I have a plan and I need to make the arrangements with you. We need to discover a way for David to join me here in Happiness. I've considered asking my chauffeur to drive him here. I trust the two of them can make the trip safely. I need your help. I don't want anyone following them or stalking my son. I'm hoping we can do this without any media exposure."

"When do you want him to leave here? Do you think we can get him there safely in the middle of the night? Or, do you want to wait until tomorrow morning? While you talk with David on the cell phone, I can call Mr. J, the chauffeur, and get his feedback."

"Thank you, that will save me some time. May I speak with David now?" She hands David the phone and takes off to call Mr. J. on the landline. Jake and his son have a quiet conversation sharing this and that. David thanks his dad for the picture of him and Lacey.

"Son, It's almost bedtime. You can go brush your teeth while I finish my conversation with Nanny. I love you, Son. We'll be together again soon."

Nanny returns to the phone and speaks with Jake. "Mr. J said he'd be happy to drive him through the night incognito. I can escort David there to care for him while Mr. J drives. He'll probably sleep the whole time but I can keep an eye on him so that Mr. J can keep his focus on the road. We talked about using a newer car at the limo company. I can drive David over to an undisclosed location. He'll drive me back to my car after we leave David at the B&B with you. I'm assuming of course, you'll drive him back home in your personal car."

Jake is pleased with Nanny's and Mr. J's suggestions. He says, "That plan should work just fine. Please pack an overnight bag for him with casual and play clothes that will be good through Sunday evening. Maybe, he'd like a few of his favorite toys. There's enough room out here for us to play catch. Please pack his glove and baseball. I would like to share the news with him."

Nanny hands David the phone and tells him, "Your Dad wants to talk you. He has good news."

"Son, how would you like to spend time with me here in Happiness? Nanny and I decided with Mr. J to drive you out here to the B&B during the night. The trip will take about three hours. You'll probably sleep through most of it. I'll have a bed made in my room waiting for you here in the B&B."

"Do you mean it, Dad? WOW. I'm excited about a new adventure. Will I get to play with Lacey, too? I miss you so much, Daddy. I'm so happy."

"I'm happy, too, Son. It should be a fun and memorable adventure for us. If everything goes as planned, I'll see you soon."

"Okay, Daddy. I can't wait to give you a big hug around your neck. Good night!"

Nanny and David go upstairs to his bedroom. They work together packing an overnight bag and his toothbrush. She also finds a bag to pack a few of his favorite toys and his baseball with catcher's mitt. He tells her that he doesn't want to take any toys. He wants to play with his Daddy and Lacey at the B&B.

Nanny smiles happily and says, "You know that's fine. Your daddy asked me to pack your baseball and mitt for a game of catch. Do you want to find them?"

David's eyes light up and he smiles so sweetly. He answers, "I would love to play catch with my Daddy. We haven't played outside together for a long time. I'll find my baseball and mitt. I think they're in a toy box in my closet."

Nanny goes to her room and prepares herself for the road trip. She calls Mr. J. and tells him, "I'm ready to meet you at our secret location. My car should be okay parked at that location for a few hours. I'll see you there in about 10 minutes."

Mr. J. says, "Ok. I'll be waiting for you. I think it's a wonderful thing for them to spend some fun time together. I'm anxious to make this reunion happen."

Nanny explains to David. "Mr. J is on his way. He'll pick us up in a few minutes at a place I know about 10 minutes from here. Can you carry the bag with your baseball and mitt? I'll carry your overnight bag."

"I've got it just fine."

Nanny locks up and secures the house. She helps David buckle up in the backseat of her car and places his bags on the seat next to him. By the time, Nanny and David arrive, Mr. J is waiting for them and standing by the open backseat door of a long limo. He helps David buckle up while Nanny settles in on a seat across from him. Mr. J loads the bags in the trunk.

Mr. J says cheerfully, "Are we ready to hit the road? Destination, Happiness and the Cotton Family Bed and Breakfast."

Both David and Nanny happily say, "Yeeesss!"

Nanny sends Jake a text. Mr. J, David and I are currently on our way to Happiness. We'll see you in a few hours. I'll text you again when we arrive in town."

Jake responds with a text, "Thanks for letting me know. Please ask Mr. J to drive carefully. I think he told me once that he's had years of experience. I'm not fond of driving at night so I admit I'm a little on edge."

Her next message, "I'll tell him but I think we'll be okay. The weather is clear, road conditions are good and he's driving a brand-new limo."

He replies, "Sounds good. I'll be waiting to hear that you've arrived in Happiness. Let me know if you have any trouble finding the B&B. We can meet in town if necessary."

Her response is a simple, "Okay!"

Mr. J drives the limo with only one stop at a gas station. A neck pillow keeps David comfortable while he's sleeping. Nanny is relaxed but not asleep. She tries extra hard to stay alert in case David needs her care.

Mr. J offers, "Would you like a cup of coffee or a cold beverage? I need a cup of coffee to go. It'll help me stay more alert behind the wheel. I see David is out like a light. Do you want a snack?"

Nanny says gratefully, "No, thank you, at this hour just a cup of water will be fine."

He pays for his cup of coffee to go and a bottle of cold water. They're on the road again.

In the meantime, Jake, Darla, Jenny, Denise and I are sitting in the den engaging in a fireside chat. The ambience is excellent for the family and friends to visit about old and new memories. They also share dreams and their future.

I ask Jake, "Would you like to sit out on the deck where it's quiet for a few minutes?"

He quietly says, "I think I'm ready for the solitude I feel, while sitting on the back deck. Are you going to join me out there?"

I answer, "I can if you want me to? I'm beginning to feel like we're old friends since you shared some of your personal life with me."

"Yes, you've been a great friend by offering your support and encouragement. You're a good listener and I really need that right now."

I want Jake to relax and just breathe in the fresh air. I encourage him, "I'll try my best to be a good listener. Feel free to talk about whatever is stressing you."

Jake shares, "I'm on stress overload with my business and family issues. I don't think that I'm ready to talk about the whole story. The greatest stress right now is wanting to know that my son is alright. It's been hard on both of us. I lost my wife and his mother to cancer about a year and a half ago. My business has been going strong but it keeps me busy with traveling around to different locations. I have a great Nanny that's loving and caring. David loves her like a Mom. I know it's not the same. He's a good kid and I wish that I could be around more often."

I don't say anything. I just let him speak and share whatever he wants to talk about. I'm a good listener.

He continues, "Not that I'm glad my car broke down by any means, but I'm glad I had the chance to meet you and your family. I'm glad I had a chance to enjoy the great outdoors and yes, I'm even glad I got to help at the café. It's a good feeling to connect with nature and recall memories of happier times. I believe that when David arrives here, we'll have a wonderful time together. What about you, Candy? How are you doing?"

I answer, "I'm fine Jake. I'm so sorry to hear about the loss of your wife and David's mom. I know how hard it is to lose loved ones."

Jake hears his phone chime. He reads the text message from Nanny. "We're in Happiness and on the road where the B&B is located. We should arrive there in a few minutes."

He sends a reply stating, "I'm waiting on the back deck. I'll meet you at the limo when you arrive. I can't wait to see my son again. I've missed him so very much!"

Chapter Nine
Happy Saturday Morning

Jake tells me, "My Nanny just sent a text letting me know they'll arrive in a few minutes. I'll need to listen for the limo driver to park out in front."

"I'll help you listen for them. Would you like for me to brew a fresh pot of coffee? The driver might need a cup before driving back to your town. When I must drive at night, I tend to drink a lot of coffee which helps me stay awake."

Jake says, "That's a very generous offer. Are you sure it's not too much trouble?"

I answer, "Not at all. I think I'll have a cup, too. What about you? Usually, I don't drink coffee this late at night but Denise and I will visit later.

Before he has a chance to answer, he hears the limousine. While walking down the steps, he says, "Yes, I'll join you for a cup of coffee and a chance to visit."

Jake hurries out to the limo and carries his sleeping son upstairs to his bedroom. He gently places David on the pull-out bed. He gives his son a goodnight kiss. The light is on in the bathroom and the door is ajar. Jake doesn't want his son to feel frightened in the dark. No telling how he might react, if he woke up in a strange bed. Then, he hurries back down the stairs to locate David's luggage.

Mr. J and Nanny carried the bags in from the car and left them at the foot of the stairs. He picks up his son's bags and takes them up to his room. He's very grateful for their help. He hurries back downstairs to greet Nanny and Mr. J. and to say thank you.

I invite the driver, Mr. J and the Nanny to come in for a visit while Jake takes care of his son. I introduce myself to them with a friendly smile.

The Nanny says, "You can call me Beth which is short for Elizabeth."

Mr. J says, "You can call me Jay!" He smiles and says, "Very nice to meet you, Candy."

I tell them, "I'm delighted to meet you, too. I brewed a fresh pot of coffee for us. If you'd like to drink a cup, we can sit here at the kitchen table and chat. Would you like a piece of apple pie with your coffee?"

Jake says with a big smile, "Yes, I would love a piece of apple pie with my coffee." He finds the paper plates and forks for all of them. He suggests that the ladies in the other room might like a piece of pie, too.

Darla went upstairs to bed earlier. I ask the ladies in the den if they'd like pie and coffee but they decline. They tell me they're close to being ready for bed. They're very relaxed and want to get a good night's sleep. Denise says, "Perhaps we'll have more time to visit tomorrow. I'll say goodnight." She stands up and gives me a hug and heads to her room upstairs.

Aunt Jen also gives me a goodnight hug and says, "I'll see you in the morning! Saturday will be a busy workday at the café." I tell them both goodnight and return to the kitchen. I see Lacey following Aunt Jen upstairs but she stretches out in front of Jake's door. He seems excited about David's presence.

Beth tells Jake, "I would love a piece of pie but not the coffee, thank you. I need a good night's sleep. I'm afraid the coffee will keep me awake all night."

I offer her a choice of several different flavors of tea instead of coffee. She decides to drink of cup of chamomile tea. We work together heating the water, finding a cup and spoon. It's so natural having her here like we've known each other for a long time. Very interesting.

While we finish our coffee, tea and pie, we sit and chat about things here and there as well as this and that. It's like a family reunion for Jake. We all feel at home although we're meeting here for the first time. Jay and Beth make eye contact and simultaneously acknowledge the time is flying by.

Jay stands up and announces their plan to leave now. He shakes hands with Jake and I with a big smile and a thank you. Beth and I exchange a goodbye hug as she says thank you to me. But while she hugs Jake, he says, "A big thank you to both you and Jay for making the trip out with David and taking good care of him." Jake smiles and says, "Safe travels. Have a good weekend with your family."

Beth tells, Jake, "I'll be in touch with you again on Sunday." Beth and Jay leave the house and depart for their return home.

It seems natural for Jake and me to work together picking up the dishes and cleaning up the kitchen area. He reaches over and touches my shoulder with a smile. He says, "Thank you very much, Candy, for everything that you've done to make my stay here so enjoyable. Thank you for the chance to spend this quality time with my son. I plan to make the very best of our time here, tomorrow." I smile back and then our eyes lock for just a moment. We feel a warm connection but the attraction is a mystery to both. We gently exchange a goodnight hug.

Jake says, "I better go check on my son and get some sleep. I plan a full day of fun with David. Good night, Candy and thanks again."

I tell him, "Goodnight, I'll see you and David in the morning. If I can do anything special to help care for him, please let me know. I'll be working at the café tomorrow. I hope to see you sometime after that. Please make yourself at home here and enjoy your Saturday." We go our separate ways. I hear Lacey walking on the stairs after Jake closes and locks his door.

It was a long busy day for me. I was sure as soon as my head rested on the pillow I'd sleep soundly. I fell fast asleep but did not sleep as sound as I usually do. I felt anxious and thought a lot about the hug between Jake and me. Well, not so much the hug but the looking deeply into each other's eyes stirred a lot of emotion.

It's Saturday morning! I'm trying to turn off my alarm but I still feel sleepy and my eyes are still half closed. Ugh! Not the best way to start a busy day! I can hear Darla busy working in the kitchen preparing her usual breakfast for our guests. I can faintly hear Lacey moving around and the voice of a child. It's a rare treat to have a child at our B&B. I'm looking forward to meeting him. He looked so cute in his birthday picture.

Although, I'm tired, I hurry and get dressed in a casual outfit for our breakfast gathering. I'll get ready for the workday after I have coffee and nourishment. I open my bedroom door and I can hear David laughing. From the top of the stairs, I can see him down on the floor playing with Lacey. They're having a fun and happy Saturday morning! Watching them play, places a big smile on my face, too.

I slowly walk down the stairs to prevent startling our young guest. As I reach the bottom step, I see Jake with his camera taking a series of photos of his son playing with Lacey. I quietly walk toward them with hopes of meeting David and a chance to say good morning to Jake.

He's smiling from ear to ear as he watches and interacts with his little son. He's having a happy Saturday morning, too. I say, "Good morning, Jake! Have you eaten breakfast? You're up earlier than I expected. Looks like you and David are having a good time here with Lacey. She's a very loving dog and I'm happy to see her receive the love David has for her."

Jake says, "Good morning, Candy. Yes, we are used to getting up early for school and a work schedule back home. Guess it's a habit we tend to keep on the weekend, too. No, we haven't eaten breakfast, yet. Darla is busy prepping the kitchen but David and I agreed to wait for you and your family. I told him all about you and your family and he's excited to meet everyone.

I ask, "Are you two ready to eat breakfast now? I'll need to eat breakfast and prepare for the workday at the café."

Jake replies, "Sure, we'll go upstairs and wash our hands really quick and will join you in the kitchen as soon as possible." He tells his son, "David, I'd like for you to meet Candy." David stands up straight and respectfully greets me like a little gentleman.

David says, "It's a pleasure to meet you. I've heard lots of nice things about you from Daddy."

I tell him, "I'm delighted to meet you, David. Welcome to the Cotton Family Bed and Breakfast in Happiness. I hope you and your Daddy enjoy your stay here."

He replies, "I've had lots of fun here already. I'm so happy to see my Daddy and he says we'll have a fun adventure this weekend. Thank you. Daddy has been taking lots of photos of us together. He can share the fun with you."

I say, "That sounds like a great idea." I smile and say, "I'll meet you in the kitchen for breakfast soon." I walk into the kitchen while Jake and his son go upstairs to freshen up.

I greet Darla with a light hug around her neck and whisper, "Thank you! You always do a great job preparing breakfast for our guests. Looks like you put forth extra effort for David. You're very sweet!"

Darla replies, "Yes, we don't have the joy of entertaining young children here very often. I think it's worth the extra time to help him feel TLC (tender loving care).

I greet Aunt Jen and Denise sitting at the table chatting while sipping on a mug of coffee. Darla, bless her heart, pours a mug of coffee for me and places it on the table next to Denise. Jake and David arrive in the kitchen while she's pouring a mug of coffee for herself. She saves it for later while she assists our B&B guests.

Jake introduces his son to the group and they are all happy to meet him. They make him feel at home. They're all so kind to each other, David feels like they're a big happy family. Darla shows him the superhero cartoon placemat that she's placed for him at the table. Jake has a chair waiting for him at the head of the table right next to his son.

Darla says, "We have all the usual breakfast items in the refrigerator and on the counters. You can either help yourself to what you want or you can let me know if you need my help.

David says, "Dad they have my favorite cereal here. Can I eat that for my breakfast?" Jake locates the cereal among the boxes set out on the counter. He picks up two bowls and two spoons. He places a bowl and spoon on the placemat for his son. The other bowl and spoon is placed on the table for himself. Jake says, "I'll have what you're having, son, just for the fun of it. How about a banana? We can share one by slicing a few pieces of it on top of our cereal. Sounds yummy!" He chuckles and his son smiles big with excitement.

He proceeds to find the milk and a grape juice box in the refrigerator. After he takes care of his son, he looks around the room and asks all the ladies if he can get anything for them. He's quite the gentleman. We all reply that we're doing okay. Everyone is seated comfortably at the table now and ready to eat their breakfast. He pours the milk on their cereal and banana slices. After returning the milk carton to the refrigerator, he grabs the coffee pot and pours refills for everyone that wants it! Jake and his son are having a very happy Saturday morning!

Chapter Ten
Fun Day Ahead

David leans in close to his Dad's ear and whispers softly, "I know you introduced us, Daddy, but who are these people."

He replies with a smile and a pat on his son's little shoulder, "You've already met Candy. Seated next to her is one of her friends by the name of Denise. Candy's Aunt Jenny is sitting at the other end of the table across from me. To her right is Darla who is Aunt Jenny's niece. Candy, Aunt Jenny and Darla are all part of the Cotton Family that owns this Bed and Breakfast. Candy owns and runs a café in downtown Happiness. We'll plan on eating lunch there together. Both Aunt Jenny and Candy will be there later today."

I ask Jake and David, "How are you doing? Did you sleep well?" I ask David, "Were you excited when you woke up this morning? I bet it was good to see your Dad again?"

David's eyes light up and says, "Yes! I was so happy to see him. I jumped out of bed right into his arms. We sat on this big bed together and talked about things. We took a few selfies to send to my Nanny, too. She likes to see pictures of me when I'm smiling. I'm so happy to be here with my Daddy. I really missed him. He says that we can have lots of fun here this weekend."

Jake replies, "Yes, I think we both slept well. I was just as happy to wake up and see my son there. I just laid there watching him sleep like a little angel. It's great to be here with him. I look forward to enjoying the outdoor activities with him today. David and I really need this quality time together. I really missed him. I can show you the pics we took if you want to see them."

I answer with a smile, "Sure, I would love to see your photos. I love to see people smiling."

Jake takes out his cell phone and shows me the selfies he took of them in the bedroom and while standing outside on the balcony this morning. They are great and it is obvious that this father and son really love each other. I offer to take their picture while they are here at the B&B. Both react with excitement. Jake and David enjoy making family photo albums together.

I ask, "Would you like a picture of the two of you here at the table?"

He replies, "Sure, may I take a picture of the Cotton Family and Denise with David for our new adventure album?"

The Cotton family and Denise agree to a photo shoot. I suggest a different background. "Maybe, a family photo in the den in front of the fireplace will be a better location. We can spread out and include Lacey next to David for your keepsake photo.'

I used his cell phone to take a couple of pics of Jake and David. Then we all moved into the den for a family photo. Jake used his digital camera to take the photos. I offered to take a picture of David and Jake in front of the fireplace, too. Jake said, "Yes, but let's include Lacey. I know that will make my son smile."

Jake gave me a quick lesson on how to operate his camera but he set it up for me to basically just point and shoot. We both laughed but it works great and captures an adorable picture.

By this time, everyone is ready to disperse and begin their workday. I tell them, "I have to get ready now to leave for the café. I need to open and be sure that everything is ready to go in time for our Saturday lunch crowd. I have employees that will arrive there soon. Will I see you and David at the café later?"

Jake answers, "We haven't made definite plans yet but I would like to bring David by the café sometime today. Maybe it will be for our lunch or dinner. I hope we'll see you there. We wish you a good day."

David walks up to me and hugs me around my waist and says, "Thank you for breakfast and fun with Lacey! Hope you have a good day." His hug stirred a lot of emotions. I'm not used to feeling love by a child. Jake gave me a wink and a smile.

I said, "I must go now or I'll be late. Have a good day!" I turned and walked up the stairs as quick as I could.

Jake sat down with David on a sofa in the den and asked, "Why did you hug, Candy?"

David thinks he's in trouble. With a sad face, he replies, "She reminds me of Mommy and Nanny. She just felt like part of my family. Candy is very nice and I think she likes you too, Daddy."

You're not in trouble, son, I just wondered why because you just met her this morning. You don't react to her like she's a stranger.

"She doesn't feel like a stranger to me. What are we going to do today? What's next? Can we go outside and walk on the beach? It looks beautiful from the balcony. Can we take Lacey for a walk and play ball with her outside? What do you want to do, Daddy?

Can we play outside together now because you said it's going to be a fun day for us."

Jake picks up his little son and hugs him tight. He tells David, "Yes, I think this will be a good time for outdoor activities. We can go upstairs and change into more casual play clothes. We'll want to be free and relax while playing with Lacey and walking on the beach. Let's stop back in the kitchen and see if Darla needs a hand. We can help her clean up our mess."

They walked into the kitchen and noticed everything is neat and tidy. The ladies have successfully put everything away and cleaned the kitchen. They checked on Lacey but did not see her around either. After changing their clothes upstairs, they walked through the back door and on the back deck.

Jake says with surprise, "Aha! There you are, Lacey!" Darla is sitting with her while taking her break and drinking a glass of cold water. He asks Darla, "Is it okay if we take Lacey out for a walk with us down by the beach. David wants to throw a ball or Frisbee for her to play with, too!"

Darla answers, "Yes, I'm sure she would love that. Aunty Jenny and Candy left for the café but Denise is lounging by the beach. Please, you two know that you can make yourselves at home. Have fun today! I've got a lot of work to do, so I'll see you later!"

Jake says, "Thank you for everything. I'll stop at a store later today for a couple of beach towels. It's a beautiful warm day. We don't swim but I think we'll enjoy splashing around in the shallow water. Hope you have a good day, Darla, see you later!"

It only took a few minutes for David to run down the steps with Lacey. They were having a fun time just running around back and forth in the yard. Jake called David over to the box of Lacey's toys. They picked out the Frisbee and a ball to play with her. They took turns tossing the toys in the air for her to catch for about 15 minutes.

Jake found Lacey's leash draped over the railing on the back deck. They hooked it on to her collar and decided to go for a walk around the lake. They did not want to disturb Denise at the beach, at least for now.

Lacey loves David! She let him lead her on the leash without any resistance. Jake thinks that is a perfect photo moment but realizes he forgot his camera. He uses his phone for a quick snapshot. While he's holding the phone in his hand, he receives a text from Beth.

She wrote, "Just checking in. Thank you for the pics that you sent this morning. My favorite is the selfie taken on the balcony with the lake in the background. Just gorgeous! I'm happy to visit with my family but I miss both of you. Hope you are having a fun day!"

He sends a quick reply, "Everything is fine. Talk soon!"

Before he's able to return the phone to his pocket, the cell phone vibrates with a call from the mechanic. He answers, "Hello, Al. So, glad to hear from you again today. How are you?"

Al replies, "I'm doing great which is why I'm calling you. Your car is repaired and ready for you to pick up. Do you want to come in to the garage this morning? I'll take my lunch break around noon."

"I'm planning on having lunch at the cafe with my son around that same time. It'll take a few minutes for us to get changed but we'll be there shortly. Thank you, Al." He ends the call and shares the news with his son. They continue their walk back to the house.

He tells David, "We need to get Lacey settled back inside and change our clothes for our trip in to town. Al is waiting for us to pick up my car. We'll eat lunch at the Café after that, okay?"

"Sounds great, Daddy! It's so fun to be here. Can we play at the beach this afternoon after lunch?"

Jake says, "Yes, I planned to shop for beach towels while we are in town. We might have a chance to do a little fishing at the end of the pier. Would you like to try that? I used to fish with my grandpa when I was about your age. We'll make plans to enjoy the rest of the day together."

They arrive at the back door and greet Darla again. Jake explains his plans to her and she takes care of Lacey. Jake and David go upstairs to freshen up and change into casual clothes for shopping and eating at the café. They anxiously buckle up in the loaner car and drive to Al's Auto Repair shop.

Al is waiting with his bill and the keys to Jake's car. He pays the bill in full and tells Al, "I filled up the gas tank to replace the fuel I used." Al said, "Thank you but you didn't have to do that." Jake says, "I know, just a way to express my gratitude for the work you did and loaning a car to me."

Jake and David walk over to where their car is parked. David says, "Daddy, it's warm enough to ride in the convertible with the top down. That would be fun."

Jake says maybe after we eat our lunch, we can ride with the top down and see a few sites around town. I also want to take some time to go shopping. Okay? You know, the café is just down the street. We'll eat our lunch there now. It's probably going to be busy on a Saturday and difficult to find a parking spot. Just a minute. I'll be right back."

Jake walks back a few steps to the garage door. Al is walking out and closing the shop. Jake asks, "Al, is it okay if we leave the car parked here and walk down to café from here?"

"Sure, I'm on my way there now. We can walk together if you would like to? Your little boy reminds me of my grandson when he was younger. He's so cute and very polite."

Jake says, "Yes, we can walk down to the café together. How about eating lunch with us? It'll be my treat. I'm grateful to you for fixing my car and for suggesting the café and B&B. I've had a wonderful time getting to know the Cotton family."

The three of them walk two blocks down the street to the Candy Cotton Café.

Chapter Eleven
Fun in The Sun

While Jake and David walked to the café with Al, they had a friendly chat. Al says, "Thank you for your generous offer to treat me to lunch, Jake. I must decline your offer because I have a prior commitment to eat lunch with my wife and family. It's my son's birthday today. Would you like to join us?"

Your invitation is tempting but it would be best if David and I try to finish our meal quickly. We have a busy afternoon planned. Thank you. Maybe we can try again the next time I happen to be passing through this lovely town,"

Al says, "By the way David, welcome to Happiness. I hope that you and your Dad will enjoy your weekend together."

David responds, "Thank you, Mr. Al. I'm glad you fixed Daddy's car so that we can go back home tomorrow."

When they arrive at the front door of the café, Jake shakes Al's hand and says, "Thank you again and we hope you have a fun celebration with your family. Maybe we'll meet again before we leave Happiness."

Al smiles and says, "Enjoy your meal and fun time with your son. Kids sure grow up fast."

They open the door and enter the crowded café. Al's family group is already seated and waiting for him. Al waves goodbye and joins their birthday celebration.

Jake spots a table in a booth. They claim it, sit and discuss what they should order for their lunch from the deli. it's a Saturday crowd, the line is moving along fast. The crowd will pick up closer to one o'clock. He wants to order something quick and get in and out to use the afternoon for fun outdoor activities.

Jakes asks, "David, let's share a club sandwich from the Deli. They sell delicious fresh baked apple pie from their bakery section. Does that sound good to you?"

"Yes, Daddy. May I have chocolate milk?"

"Ok! I have an idea. Let's order our meal to go. We can have a picnic at the city park. I noticed they have picnic tables and a playground. Then we go to the store and do a little shopping."

David's smile lights up his face, "Yay! Let's have a picnic. When we go to the store, will you please buy me a new baseball cap and sunglasses. I forgot to pack my old ones. I'm not used to spending this much time in the bright sun."

"Yes, I think I'll buy a new cap and shades for myself, too. It will be good to blend in with the people living in Happiness. Can you sit and wait here while I take time to order our meal? I'll be back as soon as possible."

The waitress sets two glasses of water on their table. She also hands David a child's placemat with a small box of crayons. The mat is printed with a couple of word games and a coloring page. He tells her, "Thank you!" She smiles!

While David waits for his Dad, he also glances up and looks around at all the new people. They're smiling and happy just like the family and friends at breakfast this morning. He spies the TV over the coffee bar and just happens to catch a news update. He sees a picture on the screen of him with his daddy. He can't hear the TV and wonders why?!

I walk over to say Hello to Jake while he's still standing in line. Aunt Jenny is working the counter with another employee. He tells me about his plan to order their meal to go and eat it as a picnic at the picnic. I'm thrilled for them to be outdoors having fun together. It's a beautiful spring day!

I see David sitting at their table looking a little upset. I walk over and say, "Hello again, David. Are you doing okay? Your Dad should be here soon. He's next up in line. What are you coloring? It's looking great!"

He reaches over and gives me a gentle hug around my neck with his little arms. He says, "Hello, Candy. I'm coloring a picture of a sailboat on the lake with some kids sitting on the fishing pier. It looks like a picture of your lake at the bed and breakfast."

I laugh and say, "Yes, it is a drawing of our lake that we printed on the placemat. I hear you and your daddy are going on a picnic for lunch. That sounds like fun!"

"Can you eat lunch with us at the park? Why is there a picture of daddy and me on the TV?"

I reply, "I would love to join you two at the park for a picnic. I'm sorry but I must work here at my café. This is my job. I don't know why you're on TV. Perhaps, you should ask your Daddy about it."

Jake walks up from behind me with his to-go-order. He must have overheard a bit of our conversation because he asks, "What is the question, David?"

"Daddy, I saw picture of us on the TV. I asked Candy why but she said I should ask you."

"Oh, okay. We can talk about that while we're at the park. Are you ready to go now, David? We need to walk back to the repair shop for the car. The park is about 5 blocks away in the opposite direction. The sun is bright and it's becoming very warm outside."

I quietly reassure Jake by sharing, "I think you'll be okay. I really don't think anyone in here really paid that much attention to the TV. The volume is muted and everyone seems to be chatting with each other."

David asks, "May I bring my picture and crayons, too?"

I nod with approval and Jake replies, "Yes. Say goodbye to Candy."

"Goodbye, Candy, we'll see you later." Jake also tells me goodbye with a friendly smile. I watch them walk toward the door and like a flash of light I get an idea. I ask them to wait for just a minute. I go to the back and grab a small tablecloth for them to use on the picnic table. I hand it to Jake and say, "You can return it later. You know David asked me if I could join your picnic. Think of me, okay?" They exchange smiles and a little laughter.

I watch them walk through the door and down the street toward their car. Aunt Jenny knows me too well. She asks me, "What's up with you and Jake? You've known each other for two days but look at each other like you are soulmates."

"Yes, it's a mystery to me. I'm not sure what I'm feeling right now. It doesn't seem possible for us to have a mutual attraction in such a short period. I need to get back to work. Do you need a break?"

Aunt Jen says, "No, not yet, after this crowd clears out, I'll need a break. It's a typical busy Saturday lunch crowd." I keep myself busy as usual and try not to be distracted by day dreams.

Jake and David arrive at the city park and locate a table close to the playground. The sounds of children laughing is music to their ears. Even the sound of the squeaky swings is a welcome springtime sound. Jake places the small cloth on the picnic table while thinking about Candy back at the café.

While Jake and David are eating, they chat quietly about the TV question. He explains to his son, "The news reporters lost track of me when my car broke down. I've been out of my usual routine and the reporters are talking about it on the TV. I really did not want them to find us and report stories about us being here. I needed some time away from work and other stress. Being here has been good for me and I wanted to enjoy it without reporters. That is why I want you to be here with me. I want us to enjoy our time here together, too. I hope no one will recognize us while we're here in Happiness."

"OH! I see! It's wonderful to be out of school and away from my usual routine, too. We don't get to spend a lot of time together at home. I'm glad we're here in Happiness."

When you're finished eating, we can wash our face and hands with hand wipes that I have in the car. We can spend some time playing on the playground. I can give you a push on the swing like the old days." They laugh!

David says, "I can swing by myself now, but I remember the old days when we used to play at the park with Mommy. I sure do miss her."

"I do, too, son! Are you ready to play? Then we must make a trip to the store for caps, shades and beach towels. We can wear cutoffs in the water but I think we might need water shoes. It's been a long time since I've gone fishing. I'm not sure what they have available for us. I guess we can figure that out later."

"Our lunch was delicious, Daddy. I need a drink of water."

"Come on with me to the car. I need to stash the table cloth and we need to clean our hands. I think there's a water fountain closer to the playground."

After they're finished at the car, they walk over to the playground. David drinks water from the fountain and heads for the swing. Jake follows and joyfully gives him a gentle push. Their laughter mingles with the sounds of the other children playing and having a good time. Jake tries out the swing next to his son. The seat is large enough but with his long legs, it's a little too close to the ground. He uses his cell phone to take a few selfies of the two of them at different locations on the playground. They're perfect pics and will add them to their new adventure family album.

They play for about a half an hour and feel the heat from the sun draining their energy. Jake suggests they take a break and rest in the shade. David says, "I feel hungry again. Can we find an ice cream store and enjoy a cone together? It's been a long time since we've done that."

Jake replies, "I think Candy has ice cream on her menu at the café. I'm not sure about the cones. Do you want to make a stop back there after we finish our shopping at a store? The lunch crowd should be gone by then. Maybe she can visit with us while we eat ice cream."

"That sounds great, Daddy. Are you ready to go to the store now?"

"Ok, let's go. There's a store a few blocks over south of here that I shopped at for my new clothes. Let's head that direction and see if we can find what we need in that store. Although it's advertised as a men's store, they might have some other items for little boys."

They arrive and right away cool off from the air conditioning in the store. David says, "Aah, that air feels so good." He sighs and breathes deeply. They walk around the store and find everything they're looking for and more. They found a section in the store for boys. David found a few new casual outfits which work well for play clothes while on vacation this weekend. They check out and drive back to the café for their ice cream treat. They look really cool with their new baseball caps and shades.

David says, "I don't think Candy will recognize us!"

"We'll see. It's good luck to find a parking spot so close to the front door. Can you please hand the tablecloth to me? We need to return it to Candy."

Chapter Twelve
Soulmates?!

I'm surprised to see Jake and David again so soon. I admit my heart felt like it skipped a beat. Although, I'm busy moving tables and chairs back in place, I walk behind the counter to wait on them personally. I ask, "How can I help you?"

David whispers to his daddy, "See, I don't think she recognizes us."

Jake laughs and says, "Hello, Candy we're looking for an ice cream treat. After we ate our lunch, we played at the playground. We also shopped at the men's store. It's very warm outside. Now, we want to cool down with a cold treat. Do you serve ice cream cones here?"

I tell him, "Yes. We also have sundaes, banana splits and malts available. What kind of ice cream cone would you like? Waffle?"

David speaks up and says, "Daddy, you like banana splits and I like sundaes. Can we have that instead of a cone? It's been a really long time."

"I agree but I'm not hungry enough to eat a banana split. I think a one scoop sundae for each of us will be good. What flavor do you want, David?"

David answers, "My favorite vanilla ice cream with chocolate sauce and a cherry on top."

Jake says, "I'd like to order a sundae for David. I'd like a sundae for myself with chocolate ice cream."

David asks me, "Can you eat an ice cream treat with us? It doesn't look very busy right now. We can show you the pictures we took at the playground. It was fun!"

"I probably have time. Is it okay with your Daddy?"

Jake smiles and says, "It's perfectly okay with me. Looks like you had a busy lunch crowd today. If you agree to take a break and visit with us, I'll make a deal with you. We'll work at setting the tables and chairs back in their proper places. We make a good team. It'll give us something to do while you prepare our ice cream snacks. Is it a deal?"

I'm blushing but I agree with their generous offer. It's an honor to accept their invitation. I prepare two sundaes with extra cherries on top for them and one like David's for myself. MmMm!

Aunt Jen surprised me! She was working back in the office but suddenly appeared beside me. She softly and sweetly says, "I see the guys are back again. I was thinking perhaps I can cover for you tonight. I suggest you follow your heart and take the rest of the day off. They leave for home tomorrow, don't they? I'd like to share my words of wisdom. If he's your soulmate, you need to know it for sure. Otherwise, after he's gone, you'll always wonder what if?"

I quietly reply, "I thought that same thing earlier today as I watched them walk out the door. It just seems so complicated. I've heard of love at first sight but never dreamed it would happen to me. I've just been too busy with other things to think about having a love life. Can you really cover for me on a busy Saturday night? Maybe, Jerry and Margaret will agree to a double shift. We can pay them extra."

"Yes, that's what I had in mind. I'll give have a chat with them now and see if that plan will work for us. Feel free to take the rest of the day off if you want to. I'll be here for you no matter what. Enjoy your ice cream and your visit! Have fun!"

I tell her, "Thank you, Aunt Jen. David is a sweet caring child. He takes after his Dad. Please let me know if they're willing to cover for me tonight."

Jake and David finished the chore, washed their hands and are now ready to eat their sundaes. We find a table in the corner by the side window away from the TV. We chat and laugh a lot. David excitedly shares the playground pics on the phone. They both look so relaxed and happy. It's a joy to see Jake without stress lines on his face.

"Daddy, let's take a selfie of the three of us eating our sundaes. I want to remember the fun time. Can I take the pic with your phone Dad? I know how to do it."

"Okay, but please be careful. Let's all huddle close together."

David takes the selfie very well. We are all smiling and our eyes are open. I tell him, "Good job, David! Now, may I take a pic of us with my phone?" Both Jake and David smile and their eyes light up. They huddle in close to me while I snap a selfie with the three of us. I want to remember the fun time, too.

Jake asks me several questions about fishing and boating at the lake. He says, "Darla told me that there is a small boat and fishing gear available at the B&B to use at the lake. Is it okay if David and I check it out when we leave here? Or should I wait until after you are home to help us? I was hoping we could enjoy the lake today because we have to leave for home tomorrow."

"I can tell you that the rowboat belongs to me but I let our guests use it. I inherited it from my father. It doesn't get a lot of use except during the summer weekends. It's in good shape. We have life jackets that are probably in good condition. We'll have to double check that along with the fishing gear. I'm not sure what you'll use for bait. I haven't used a fishing pole since my Dad passed. I've seen people fishing at the lake but didn't pay attention to what they used for baiting their hooks."

"Darla did not share how I can access the boat. I didn't think I would be interested until David arrived. Now, I imagine we would enjoy the new experience of a boat ride out on the lake. I didn't ask her about the fishing gear either. Should we wait until this evening or can we explore the storage room without you? You can trust us to be careful and to take care of your treasures."

David asks, "May I have a box of crayons please? I would like to color this picture while you two are talking about grownup things." We all smile at each other.

I leave the table and find a box of crayons and a clean placemat for him. I take a few minutes to check in with Aunt Jen. She gives me an okay sign with a thumb up and says, "We've got you covered." I tell her, "Ok, I think this will work out perfectly. I'm going to take off soon. Thank you, Aunt Jen. I'll share more with you later."

While returning to the table, I overhear David and Jake talking about inviting me to join them on a boat. It was exhilarating to feel accepted by them in a loving way.

I return to my chair and hand the crayons and placemat to David. He says, "Thanks! This picture looks like the den inside your house." I tell him, "Yes, it is. You have a good eye."

Jake shares, "David and I were talking while you were away. We want to invite you to share a boat ride with us. You won't have to do any of the work. Just relax and have fun with us. You're always working very hard long hours just like I do. We think you deserve a night off for a little fun with us. Is that possible? Maybe I can cookout something in your backyard patio by the beach."

"I would like that very much, Jake. Thank you, David for suggesting it to your Dad. I would be delighted to take the night off and join you for an outdoor adventure at the lake. I've already made the arrangements with Aunt Jen. I'm free to go at any time now."

Jake asks me, "What would you like to eat for our picnic supper? I'll need to make a shopping list and stop at the grocery store. David and I can eat whatever you choose."

David says, "I like hot dogs with mustard. Can you cook hot dogs on the grill?"

I reply, "We can use my food at the B&B. We don't keep very much on hand except for breakfast food. But it's available if we want it for our picnic. I'd enjoy shopping at the grocery store with you. After you complete your list, I can help you find the items quicker because I'm more familiar with the store."

Jake gratefully says, "Thank you, Candy, I'm delighted you are free to join us. Both David and I enjoy your sweet disposition and your enjoyable company. I haven't cooked on a grill for several years. Are you up to helping me succeed with this project? We'll have to play it by ear. I know that we can have fun together if it works out as planned."

David is watching us with a smile as Jake gently touches my shoulder. He reaches across the table and places his little hand on top of mine. "He says, "I'm glad we met you, Candy."

I say, "I'm glad I met you, too!" I continue to tell Jake, "Whenever you're ready to go grocery shopping, let me know. We can all go to the store in my car."

David asks, "Daddy, can we ride in our car with the top down now?"

"That's okay with me." Then he asks me, "Would you like to go for a ride in our convertible with the top down?" They laugh with excitement.

I reply, "It's a beautiful warm day for a ride in a convertible. The grocery store is about a mile away. I can leave my car parked here, if you'll bring me back to pick it up afterwards."

Jake says, "Not a problem! I think we can talk more about our menu in the car and while shopping. I really enjoy attempting impromptu activities." He stands up and encourages David to head for the front door. He follows close behind. I walk quickly to the back office and grab my purse. I also let Aunt Jen know that we're leaving.

Their car is parked close to the door which saved time for us to settle in. Jake put the top down with great ease. David is sitting in the backseat smiling from ear to ear. He is genuinely happy. I feel great joy as I sit down on the front passenger seat. My hair is cut short for convenience sake so I don't have to worry about a scarf.

When we arrive at the grocery store, a few people recognize me and greet us with a friendly smile. They appear to be surprised to see me out and about with my guests. Fortunately, most people in Happiness do not gossip because they're happily living their own lives.

We make our way through the store in a short period. Between Jake's list and our sharing freely, we ended up with a great selection of picnic food for our supper. I ask Jake to take me to the Café before driving back to the B&B. But they convince me to stay with them in the convertible until later. We need to get to the B&B as soon as possible to put the perishables away in the refrigerator.

We arrive at the house and Darla is there excited to see us. She not only finished the household cleaning which is her job but also finished her college level homework. She's free and planning to lounge at the beach this evening. I haven't seen Denise since breakfast.

I ask Darla, "Do you know where and what Denise might be up to?"

Darla replies, "Yes, she left you a note. She said, "I have to check out early and return home to my family and business. I'll stop in for a visit the next chance I get to drive through Happiness."

"Thanks, Darla. I'll read the note later. I took the night off from the café. Jake and David invited me to join them on a boat ride out on the lake this evening.

Then we plan to grill out. We have enough food for you, too, if you want to join us."

Darla says, "Thanks for the offer. I think I'll pass. Go ahead with your plans. Sounds like fun but I'm really exhausted. I want a chance to rest and relax on a lounge chair by the beach. I've heard people say that It's 'a great way to recharge my batteries'."

Chapter Thirteen
Love Is in The Air

Jake and I chat while we put away our groceries. We decide to take the boat out on the lake before we cook our supper. He says, "I bought new shorts and shirts today. David and I need to change into more appropriate casual play clothes."

I tell him, "I'm going to change into more appropriate play clothes, too! It's been a long time since I've been on the boat and engaged in outdoor activities. I'll do that now and I'll meet you back here soon." Our eyes lock again and my heart beats faster.

I slip away to my room and find a nice springtime outfit that will be perfect for our time out in the boat and sitting at the picnic table. My shades and sun hat match perfectly. Because I don't own a pair of water shoes, I slip on a pair of canvas shoes that will fare well on the beach.

While waiting in the kitchen for Jake and David, I pack a thermos of cold water and plastic cups to take out on the boat. David runs full of energy down the stairs ahead of Jake. He looks so very cute. Lacey hurries over to greet him by licking his face. Her tail is wagging hard and fast which makes David laugh. They're both happy to see each other.

When Jake arrives in the kitchen, he looks relaxed and very handsome. He has his camera in hand and ready for the new adventure. He asks, "Okay, Candy, what's next on our schedule? Are you ready to get started on our boat ride? By the way, you look beautiful."

I smile and say, "Thank you. I'm ready to set up the boat for our ride. I'll show you where the boat and boat supplies are stored. We need to try on the life jackets. Please don't let me forget to bring the thermos of cold water with us on board."

Jake finds a life jacket just the right size for David. He's eight years old but tall for his age. Jake and I can choose from several adult size jackets. We wear the newer less worn jackets for ourselves. The lake isn't very big nor is it real deep in some places but it's better to be safe than sorry.

I help Jake drag the boat out alongside the fishing pier. We decide to launch the boat from that location because it's easier and safer for David to board. The weather is perfect and the lake is calm. There's a sweet taste in the air.

Jake sweetly says, "You can sit back and relax, while I do all of the work."

David says, "Daddy please take a picture for our album. I want to remember the fun time." Jake takes out his cell phone and uses his camera for a couple of pics. I also take a couple of pics with my cell phone. David's not the only one that wants to remember the fun time.

David asks, "What is the name of this lake, Candy?"

"My daddy owned this lake with our house. He called it, 'Cotton Family Lake'." I also say, "Oh, look! Darla is waving at us. I want to take her picture, too."

Jake rows the boat out to the middle of the lake. He drops the anchor for a few minutes while he takes several pictures with his camera. The beauty of nature is very appealing and he wants to capture it. We witness several fish jumping out of the water. There's a school of fish swimming close by. David is very excited to see them!

The sun is starting to set creating beautiful colors in the sky. I suggest that we probably should head back to the beach now. Because the sun is setting now, it'll be too dark to eat our picnic dinner outside.

Jake agrees and rows the boat back to the pier. I step out onto the pier and then I help David get out safely. I tell Jake that it's okay to leave the boat tied up to the pier overnight. Tomorrow, might be a good day for another boat ride.

I show Jake where the grill, charcoal and other supplies are stored. I leave that job in his capable hands. I suggest, "We can eat at the table on the back deck. It's going to be too dark to eat at a picnic table on the beach now.

He says, "That's fine. I'll leave that job in your capable hands." We slightly shake our heads, He smiles so sweetly and looks like he wants to kiss me. It scares me a little bit. I feel like I want him to kiss me. I'm not sure about these new feelings. I'm wishing that they could stay here longer.

I wash my hands before I go to work in the kitchen. While I prep the food, David is playing ball with Lacey in the backyard close to Jake. I can smell the fire burning charcoal in the grill. We bought hot dogs and chips for David. Jake and I chose steak. The corn on the cob will be roasted for all of us. We also have a fresh fruit salad and a fresh vegetable salad on our menu.

I spread the tablecloth on the table on the deck. I set the table with real plates, silverware and napkins. It feels like a special occasion to me. I hope it feels that way to them, too.

I carry the meat platter and a separate plate with three ears of corn out to Jake. I ask him, "What would you like to drink with dinner?"

He answers, "If there's sweet tea in the refrigerator, that sounds refreshing. I think it would be best for David to drink milk with his meal."

I reply, "That sounds refreshing to me, too. If there's not, I'll make a fresh pitcher of sweet tea."

He asks, "How do you like your steak? I like mine cooked medium well done."

"That's fine with me. I'll go check on the tea and prepare the salads."

He says, "It won't take long for the meat and corn to cook. Would you like David to help with the fruit salad?"

"He's having fun with Lacey. It's okay. It won't take long to prep the salads. The table is set and waiting for the meal to be served."

I return to the kitchen and prep both the fruit and the vegetable salads. I don't usually eat very much for supper. But David is still a growing boy who needs more nourishment. I'm sure that Jake has worked up an appetite rowing the boat.

While I finish the final touch on the table, Jake tells me that the grilled food is ready to eat. David flies past us, rushing in to wash his hands. Jake washes his hands at the kitchen sink. He pours the drinks into the glasses for our meal. I have already placed condiments and other food items on the table. Jake and I sit down with David between us.

David says, "WOW! Daddy? Candy? LOOK UP! I've never seen so many stars in the sky. All those twinkle lights look so beautiful! The moon looks like a bright shining ball. Look at the light sparkle on the lake."

Jake and Candy look up, while David shares his joy about the stars and the moon. Out in the country, when the weather is clear like it is now, the stars in the sky appear bigger and brighter. In the city, there are too many lights which obscure the beauty of a moonlit and star filled sky.

Jake snaps a few photos of the three of them seated at the table and several of the nature scenes that surround them. Great memories!

I place spikes at the ends of each corn cob. The spikes are designed to make a little handle to hold the cobs firmly. It's fun watching David tackle the challenge of biting into the corn. Both Jake and David are so cute! They seem to like fresh corn as much as I do. Before we're finished eating, David's eyes are really drooping. He looks very sleepy and worn out by the full day of activities.

Jake says, "Son, are you doing okay? Did you get enough to eat? You look like you might fall asleep at the table. I think we better head upstairs. You can take a quick shower and go to sleep in your bed now. I hope you had a fun day. I sure had a fun day with you."

David replies, "Yes, Daddy, I'm very sleepy. Can you carry me upstairs? I had a fun day with you, Daddy. I also had a fun day with Candy and Lacey."

Before Jake picks him up, David, reaches over to hug me goodnight! His Dad stops him and says, "You can wait to hug, Candy after we get you cleaned up, okay?"

I laugh and say, "It's okay. After he's clean, he'll be ready to fall asleep in his bed." I reach out to him and accept his hug. I tell him, "Goodnight David. I really enjoyed the fun time we had together. I'll always remember your visit with us at the B&B and the café. Have sweet dreams."

Jakes scoops up David in his loving arms and carries him upstairs. Lacey follows them and stretches out in front of the door. I can hear the shower running. I go to work clearing off the table and cleaning up the aftermath of our picnic on the deck. Also, the kitchen looks like a small twister hit it. While David is upstairs, I clean the kitchen and then move to the den. I light a fire in the fireplace just for the sake of sitting in there to relax. It's been a long busy day with my emotions playing on a roller coaster. I take this time to collect and sort my thoughts.

Everyone is quiet in the house now. Darla and Aunt Jen are in their rooms probably sleeping by now. They were tiptoeing around us earlier trying not to disturb our special time together. Because Jake didn't tell me goodnight, I'm assuming he might return to the kitchen after David is settled in. I'm close to calling it a night because I feel sleepy and my eyelids are heavy. I take a few minutes to read the note Denise left for me.

Jake smells the wood in the fireplace burning. He barrels down the stairs and rushes into the den as if there's an urgent need to find me. He says, "Ohh! I was hoping you didn't leave for your bedroom. I want a chance to thank you for everything you did to make this day special for David and me. Thank you so very much!"

He sits down on the sofa next to me. He continues, "It's been years since I've slowed down and enjoyed family time. I've spent most of my time and energy on my business trying to be sure that David has the security of a quality life. Meeting you here in Happiness has opened my eyes. David seems to adore you, too! Financial security is important but I can see the need for a healthy balance. We need fun quality family together, too. I've been taking our life way too serious and the stress of it has been weighing heavy on us."

I say, "I understand what you're saying. I too have invested all my time and energy on my business wanting financial security. I've taken very little time for myself. I agree with you now about the need to have a healthy balance. I'm very grateful to you and David coming into my life. The fun day we shared has also opened my eyes. I never realized how much I long for a family of my own, until today. I adore David, also. Thank YOU for everything."

Our eyes lock once again. This time it feels like he's staring deeper into my eyes. I feel like I can see deep into his soul. The dancing flames in the fireplace and the sound of crackling wood create a romantic ambience in the den. It's just the two of us now. He lovingly and sweetly leans in to kiss me. This time, I lean in gently and our lips meet. I hope we don't regret this moment in the morning. For now, we share several very passionate kisses.

Chapter Fourteen
A Storm Rolls In

Lacey unexpectedly appears in the room. She's whining low but lets out a short quick bark directed at Jake. We simultaneously reach over and pat her head. We ask, "What's wrong, Lacey? Are you okay?" She acts as though she wants us to follow her. We get up and follow her lead to the back door. It's past time for her usual night time walk. I grab her leash and attach it to her collar. Jake follows us out the back door.

He says, "This will give me a chance to clean the grill. I didn't take time earlier because it needed to cool down. It's cool now." After Jake cleans the grill, He spies me waiting and watching him from the deck.

Jake thinks, *'The moonlight in her hair creates golden streaks which is beautiful. I hope we don't regret sharing those kisses in the morning. She is so sweet, loving to David and she is so beautiful. The attraction I feel is just irresistible. I need to sort through and get in touch with my real feelings. I don't want anyone to get hurt.'*

I open the door and let Lacey enter the kitchen. I quietly close the door behind her. I'm ready to call it a night but want a chance to share my thoughts with Jake. He walks up the steps on the deck and stands beside me. I'm looking out over the lake trying to relax and breathe in the fresh night air.

He says, "I need to go in and wash my hands."

I tell him, "I need to go to bed and get a good night's sleep. I must work at the café tomorrow. Aunt Jen did a great job covering for me today but our employees need a day off, too. I'll say goodnight. See you in the morning. Sleep well."

We open the door and walk inside. He goes to the utility room to wash his hands at the sink. I walk to the den to check the fire in the fireplace. It was already burning low when we left it to walk Lacey. It's burned out and safe for me to go to bed.

We end up meeting at the bottom of the stairs. We exchange a quick gentle goodnight hug. He says, "Goodnight, Candy, I'll see you in the morning."

He follows me up the stairs. At the top of the stairs I turn left and walk down the hallway to my bedroom. He turns right and walks down to his bedroom. He takes one last glance in my direction trying not to trip over Lacey. He quietly opens his bedroom door. David is out like a light. It's a comfort watching him sleep so peacefully with a smile on his face. Jake thinks, *I haven't seen him this happy for a long time.*

Jake sits on the edge of the bed and tries to collect his racing thoughts and feelings. He needs to get a good night's sleep because tomorrow will be a busy day. He plans to make the return trip with David back to their house in their hometown. He changes and freshens up before snuggling into his bed for the night.

I'm lying in bed wide awake thinking about Jake's plan to leave tomorrow. Now, I know for sure that I'll really miss him and David. I'm thankful for the time we've had together. I must sleep so that I can perform my duties at my cafe in a professional way.

A thunderstorm rolls in during the night and causes Lacey to bark when the crack of lightning and thunder are loud. Everyone in the house is awake now but no one gets up. They all snuggle up and stay in the warmth and comfort of their bed. Fortunately, David sleeps through it.

An hour or so after the storm passes through, Darla is up and working in the kitchen. She's setting the table, brewing coffee and doing other chores to prepare for breakfast. After the breakfast meal is prepped, she takes Lacey for a morning walk outside. When she returns, she has a hunch that everyone is sleeping in. There are no sounds of running water or footsteps on the floor. She realizes how unusual this is.

She pours a cup of coffee and sips it while waiting for her family and the guests to show up. She glances at the clock and decides she should check on her Aunt Jen. Before she reaches her Aunt's bedroom door, Jake and David open their door. When they walk out and see her, they say, "Good Morning, Darla!"

Darla says, "Good morning, Jake and David. I'll be down in the kitchen again after I check on Aunt Jen. Then, I pop out of my room to their surprise. I'm feeling bewildered. I ask, "Darla, what's up?" She replies with a smile, "It's getting late. You and Aunt Jen are usually up and eating breakfast by now. I was concerned so I came upstairs to check on her. I'm glad you're doing okay, too. I've prepped the kitchen for our breakfast as usual."

I reassure her by saying, "I had a late night last night and the storm kept me awake. I'm tired and moving a little slower than usual. I'll be down for breakfast in a minute. I'll check on Aunt Jen so that you can take care of our guests, okay?"

She replies, "Great idea, Candy!" She walks down the stairs followed by Jake and David. Darla assists them in locating dishes and necessary items to prepare pancakes and sausage for a special treat today. We go out of our way to make Sunday morning breakfast special for our family as well as our guests.

I knock on Aunt Jen's door and she weakly replies, "Come in." I open the door slightly enough to peek in and see if she is okay. She says, "Oh, Candy. I'm not sure what that storm brought with it, but I'm not feeling well this morning. I feel feverish and don't want to get out of bed. Will you be okay at the café today? Can you cover for me?"

"What can I do to help you this morning? Do you need help getting out of bed? Are you hungry or thirsty?" I walk over by the bedside and lovingly hold her hand.

She replies, "No, it would be better I think if you save your time and energy for the café today. I really appreciate your hard work there. I know firsthand how difficult it is for you to keep it running smoothly. I'll just rest until Darla is free. She has a lot more time around here to assist than you have. Will you please let her know that I'll appreciate her help later this morning?"

"Okay, I'll respect your wishes. I love you, Aunt Jen. Please get lots of rest and feel better soon. I'll check back with you before I leave for the café. When you're feeling better, I'd like to have a long talk with you. I need more of your wisdom."

She laughs, "Sure, dear one. I'd love for you to share your story with me about yesterday's adventure."

"Ok, I'll go for now while you rest more. See you later."

I leave her room and find Darla in the kitchen. I share with her the news about Aunt Jen. She says, "Oh, no. I'm so sorry to hear she's not feeling well. I'll be happy to check in on her and take care of her needs as soon as possible."

I tell her, "She's resting right now. A little later in the morning will be a good time to check in on her. I'm running late. I need to eat a quick breakfast and get ready for work. No time to play today. I'll need energy to do my work and cover for Aunt Jen at the café."

David asks, "Candy, would you like pancakes and sausage for your breakfast? Darla and Daddy cooked them. They let me have fun adding chocolate chips to a few of them. I added blueberries to a few of them for Darla. That's the way she likes them. What kind of pancakes do you like?"

While Jake pours coffee in a mug for me, I reply. I'm sorry David, I don't have time to sit down and eat them this morning. I'll sit down while I drink my coffee and eat some fresh fruit. There's leftover fruit salad from last night. That will work perfectly."

Jake and David are nearly finished eating their breakfast. I ask them, "What are your plans for today? From the sound of the storm last night, I'm thinking it's wet and muddy outside today. I hope you find something fun to do together before you leave on your return trip to your hometown."

Jake replies, "We haven't taken time to discuss our plans for this morning. But if everything is wet and muddy, we probably won't be able to play outside together. We'll have to figure out something before we leave here."

David says, "I've already had lots of fun. I'll always remember you, Candy. I wish that we didn't have to leave today. I don't have school tomorrow, Daddy. Can we stay another night? Maybe the sun will dry up the mud and we can have fun this evening."

Jake responds, "I know you don't have school but I've been away from my office longer than expected. First the business trip and then the car trouble. I really need to get back and make sure that things are running smoothly. I've kept in touch via email and phone calls but I really need to see for myself."

David tells me, "Nanny called Daddy this morning. She even asked to talk to me. She wants us to know how much she misses us. Her family celebration is over so she's waiting back at our house for us to come home. I like Nanny but not as much as I like being here with you, Candy, and your family. I'm going to miss you very much!" I see tears form in his eyes. His daddy reaches over and dries them.

That pulled at my heart strings which made me dry my eyes. Out of the corner of my eye, I noticed Jake dry a tear from his eye, too. He looks like the tears sting. With that, I say, "I'm sorry, but I've got to get ready to go to work. I'll be sure to say goodbye before I leave. Please enjoy the rest of your breakfast."

I hurry up the stairs and prepare for the workday ahead. While brushing my hair, I notice that my eyes are puffy and still teary. I rush to the sink and splash cold water on my face to reduce the swelling. It doesn't seem to be helping because I'm feeling very emotional. These feelings are so new to me, I just don't know how to process them.

I do know that I don't want to show up at work with swollen red eyes and feeling drained. I opt to put on a happy face. I use a little more makeup than usual to conceal as much of my sadness as possible. I take a quick trip down the hall to check on Aunt Jen. She seems to be feeling a bit better after a longer rest but I encourage her to rest more. I don't think she should push herself. I'd rather see her rested, happy and up on her feet when I return home.

I pass Jake and David while they're sitting out on the deck with Lacey. The ground is still water soaked and muddy. They're hoping the sun will dry up the rain soon. Lacey is happy stretched out at their feet. I didn't see Darla but I'm in a rush to get to work on time. I'll give her a call later and ask her for an update on Aunt Jen.

As I turn and walk down the steps, I tell Jake and David, "Goodbye and good luck on your trip back home. I hope you can make time for another trip to Happiness sometime soon. I hope that we'll meet again. I don't get off work until after the supper hour. It usually isn't very busy on a Sunday night but I often have a busy lunch hour. I've got to run."

Chapter Fifteen
Tears of Joy

I disappear around the corner of the house but I'm able to hear David say, "Daddy? Is Candy okay? She looks and sounds very upset. She was talking so fast, I couldn't understand what she said to us."

"It's okay, David. I think she's just in a hurry because she's running late for work. We'll go to the café and eat lunch before we leave for home this afternoon. We'll have a chance to say goodbye to her while we're there. In the meantime, let's slip on our water shoes. I can see from here that the boat at the pier needs attention. Do you want to help me take care of it for Candy?"

David replies, "The skies are clear now. I hope we can have fun out here today before we leave. I don't think we'll have time to go fishing today. Maybe we can spend time in Happiness during our summer vacation."

After they put on their water shoes upstairs in their bedroom, they walk down the stairs to take care of the boat by the pier. They run into Darla in the kitchen while she's preparing a food tray with coffee to take upstairs to Aunt Jenny. Jake asks, "Is your Aunt feeling better? Is there anything that I can do to help you?"

Darla responds, "My Aunt is feeling much better. She seems to be resting comfortably. Hopefully, she'll feel a lot better after she eats this healthy meal. She's a strong lady but she's also a very hard worker. The workload on the weekends often wears her out. I can't think of anything you can do to help me or my Aunt. If you're planning to eat lunch at the café, maybe you can assist Candy if she needs it. I know we all appreciate your willingness to give us an extra hand. Thank you so much for your generosity."

"After you care for your Aunt, may we sit down and have a chat? I've been thinking about other ways that I might offer my assistance to the Cotton Family. Until then, David and I will be outside trying to rescue the boat. Last night's storm really tossed it around and it's full of water."

Darla says, "Thank you for your help once again. I'll let you know when I'm free to take a break. We can chat over a cup of coffee in the kitchen or out on the deck."

David and Jake walk over to the beach with a bucket that they found in the storage shed. They can hear a funny squishy sound coming from their water shoes. David laughs and has fun stomping around on the sand. Lacey is David's constant companion while Jake works on the boat.

One of the oars floated out of the boat and washed ashore. The second oar is still securely attached to the side. Jake uses the bucket to drain most of the rain water. He unties the rope that secures the boat to the pier. He works hard at pulling the boat up to the beach. David spies his Daddy working hard to tip the boat over. He rushes over to help because he thinks it looks like fun. The ground is too wet and muddy to drag the boat back to the shed. He leans the boat up on its side up against a nearby tree. It needs to air dry on the inside before storing it away in the shed. David picks up the oar on the beach and leans it up against the tree.

Jake looks around see if the storm caused any damage. He's willing to help them while he has the free time. David wants to play ball with Lacey. Lacey doesn't like walking where it's muddy and splashing in the rain puddles. Jake suggests, "We can take her for a walk on the paved trail if it's okay with Darla."

David says, "Let's go ask her and find Lacey's leash. Okay? I like walking around the lake with her. She likes me, too, doesn't she Daddy?"

While walking back to the house from the beach, we notice Darla opening the door and stepping out on the deck. When we reach the deck, Darla says, "I can take a break now. Would you like a cup of coffee? Is there anything else I can get for you and David?"

Jakes says, "A cup of coffee sounds great. There's a chill in the air. David and I need to wash our hands and change our clothes first. We're going to the café soon for our lunch meal. David can have a glass of water, if he's thirsty. We'll be eating lunch soon. We'll join you out here soon."

Jake and David rush up the stairs to clean up from their outdoor work and play. They change their clothes and shoes for their lunch at the café. They rush back down the stairs to meet with Darla on the back deck.

David asks, "Can I play with Lacey inside while you have a grownup talk?"

Darla replies, "If it's okay with your daddy, it's okay with me. But please try to play quietly while Aunt Jenny is resting in her room."

Jake says, "It's okay with me. Play with Lacey quietly out of respect for Aunt Jenny.

Jake follows David and Lacey into the kitchen. He finds two coffee mugs. He pours a cup for Darla and one for himself. Then he sees Aunt Jenny carrying her food tray and setting it by the sink. She says, "Hello, Jake how are you doing today? I could sure use a coffee refill. Do you mind pouring some of that coffee into my mug, too?" She smiles and says, "Thank you!"

Jake responds, "I'm fine. How are you? Are you feeling better?" He refills her coffee mug and hands it to her. "Darla and I are going to drink our coffee out on the deck. Would you like to join us? I asked her to chat with me while she's taking a break."

Aunt Jenny answers, "I'm feeling a lot better but I would prefer staying indoors where it's warm. I'll stay in and visit with David and Lacey while I drink my coffee."

"Okay, I'll go out to chat with Darla now and I hope we'll see you again soon. We're going to eat our lunch in the café before we leave on our road trip."

Aunt Jenny encourages David to play with Lacey in the den. She wants to sit by the fireside and drink her coffee. Aunt Jenny makes a small fire in the fireplace just to take the chill out of the air. The large den is also a safe place for David to play with Lacey.

Jake delivers a mug of coffee to Darla and asks, "Do you use sugar or cream in your coffee?" She replies, "No, I drink my coffee straight. Thank you."

Jake asks, "Did you hear your Aunt Jenny is up and walking around? She brought her tray down. She's drinking coffee in the den visiting with David and Lacey. She looks and sounds like she's feeling okay. I hope she continues to feel better."

Darla says, "No, I didn't hear her in the kitchen. My break time is just about over. I want to check on her before I get to work on my household chores. I didn't want to run the vacuum cleaner while she was sleeping. I've got lots of work to do today including homework for my college classes."

"That's what I want to talk about with you, Darla. I appreciate your hard work around the B&B. You have shown me lots of kindness. You serve your guests with deep sincerity. I would like to offer you a well-deserved gift from David and me. I'd like to offer you $20,000 dollars to help you pay for your college classes. I'd like to see your dreams come true. I believe you will use it wisely."

Darla's jaw drops and her eyes light up. She feels speechless and sort of blankly stares at Jake. She can hardly believe what she heard. She politely asks, "What? Did I hear you correctly? I was just doing my job. I try to treat all our guests with respect and TLC. We want them to be happy and hope they will want to come back again and again. We value our guests. Are you sure? We hardly know each other."

Jake laughs and says, "Yes, I'm sure. Like I said, I think you deserve a chance to make your dreams come true. I haven't said much about myself but I can assure I have the money to help pay for your college classes. Will you accept it? We've given generously to various charities so please know the money is not a problem. David and I would really feel good knowing that we are giving back to the loving Cotton Family. We'll want to come back again and again. We've had a memorable time here."

Darla blushes but feels receiving his gift is the right thing to do. It seems that he's truly happy to give financial gifts. She says, "I really don't know what to say. Thank you is a good start but I don't know how to express my deep feelings of gratitude. I will accept and I promise that I will spend the money wisely. I've been working hard on my studies and I'm on the dean's list. I'm very grateful that I can continue my studies toward my career goals."

Jake says, "Great! I'm very happy that you will accept our gift to you." He takes out his checkbook and writes the check on the spot. He hands it to her with great joy.

Darla says, "Is it okay if I share the news with Aunt Jenny and Candy today?"

Jakes answers, "Yes, I'm planning to write a check for each one of them, also. It's just one way to say thank you to the Cotton Family for all that you have done for David and me. Let's go chat with Aunt Jenny in the den."

Darla walks ahead of Jake and sits down on the sofa next to her Aunt. She shows her aunt the check and softly explains, "This is a gift from Jake and David for my college classes."

Aunt Jenny dries tears of joy from her eyes and gives Darla a big hug. She tells Darla, "That will come in handy because tuition at your college is a high price. I'm proud and happy for you." She adds, "Thank you Jake and David for the gift that you've given to Darla."

Both Jake and David say, "You're welcome!" David doesn't know the amount of the check but knows that his Daddy likes to give people gifts to help others in need.

Darla says, "I've got lots of work to do. I'm running behind but, I'd like to run over to the bank before it closes. I want to deposit this check in my savings account. Is that okay, Aunt Jenny?"

Aunt Jenny says, "Yes, of course. That's a wise thing to do! See you later."

Darla reaches out to shake Jake's hand and wishes him a safe trip. He reaches back and tells her, "I hope to see you later." She shakes hands with Jake and with David before heading out the back door to her car.

Jake says, "Now, just as I told Darla, I want to offer you the same to help you with the Bed and Breakfast. I know that you will use it wisely. I trust that you will make the best choices for the B&B. It's been a great blessing to David and me. We've really enjoyed our stay here. We keep wishing that we could stay here longer. We hope to return during the summer for a vacation."

Aunt Jenny cries more tears of joy. She says, "It's hard for me to accept your gift but even harder for me to reject it. I admit it will help me take care of the B&B. We came up a little short this year when I had to pay the taxes. I've been giving a lot of thought about retiring but I know that Darla and Candy are still counting on my help. We're family and I can't quit on their needs. I want to be here for them. We take care of each other from time to time. Thank you so very much for your generous giving spirit. I'll always be grateful. I hope that you'll make it back here during the summer. Thanks to both you and David for this wonderful gift."

Chapter Sixteen
Spring Vacation

"You're welcome, Aunt Jenny. David and I plan to eat lunch at the café before leaving for home this afternoon. We need to finish packing up the car and leave here for the now. Time is flying by! We're hoping to have a chance to visit and say goodbye to Candy before we leave Happiness.

Would you like to join us for lunch? Or would you like for us to order a meal to go for you?" He pulls out his checkbook and writes out another $20,000 check. This time it's made out to Jennifer Cotton. He hands the check to her while waiting for her answer.

She says, "No, I'm good. I'll wait until Darla returns from the bank and then we'll eat our lunch together. I'm not feeling up to going out and about. I need to deposit my check but I'll ask Darla to take care of it for me.

"I really wish you a safe and happy trip. We'll miss you and David. You brought a lot of sunshine to our lives. You two are I angels visiting us here on earth. We'll always be grateful for meeting you and the time we've shared together. You'll always be welcome to visit with us for an extended time if you want. It's amazing that you and David feel like part of our family in the short span of a few days."

While Aunt Jenny is still seated on the sofa, David gives Aunt Jenny a goodbye hug around her neck. She pats his back and whispers in his ear, "Thank you for the fun time I've had with you. Hope to see you and your Dad again soon. Good luck at school. Bye, David!"

She stands up to exchange a goodbye hug with Jake. She pats him on his back and softly whispers in his ear, "I don't have the words to thank you enough. You've changed our lives. I know Candy is sad knowing that you two are leaving here. Take care! Bye, Jake!"

David is down on his knees giving Lacey hugs around her neck and pats her back several times. He stands up while patting her on the head and says, "Bye, Lacey! I'm going to miss you!"

Jake and David go upstairs and gather together the last of their personal items from their room. Jake carried down the larger suitcases earlier in the morning. Darla has returned home from the bank. They happen to meet in the parking lot just in time to say goodbye. She hurries over to their car to wish them a safe trip. Jake and David also give her goodbye hugs.

They're anxious to see Candy before they leave Happiness. David is hungry for lunch. Jake is experiencing butterflies in his stomach. He's struggling with mixed emotions and doesn't feel ready to leave Happiness quite yet. He feels a strong desire to spend more time with his son and Candy in this lovely town. His office and business still need his attention. There's a flood of thoughts and emotions that he's dealing with now. Trying to balance his need for both a business and family life is very difficult.

David is sitting in the backseat with tears rolling down his face. He understands the need to return home and go to school. Unfortunately, he feels the heartache of leaving Happiness and the chance for more fun with his Daddy. He misses the family closeness he senses with the Cotton family. Especially, the sweet loving TLC that the family displayed to him. He feels an attachment to Lacey which made it difficult for him to walk away.

Jake pulls out his clean handkerchief and hands it back to David. He doesn't know what to say. They'll have an easier time chatting when his Daddy is not driving the car. David dries his eyes and tries to hide his sadness with a smile. They've arrived at the café. Jake parks the car but just sits lost in thought and gripping the steering wheel for a few minutes. David asks, "Daddy are you okay? You look very sad. I'm feeling very sad, too. Do you wish we could stay in Happiness longer, too? I wish that we could live in Happiness."

"Yes, I'm okay. I am sad. Maybe, we can live in Happiness. I've been thinking about it. Are you sure that you would like to leave your friends back home and move to a new home here in Happiness? We can make frequent trips back there for you to visit with them. Or they can visit with you if they travel here for their vacation."

David says, "I don't want you to be sad, Daddy. I love you and I know you love me. I just want to be with you always. I have been happy since we came here because I got to spend lots of fun time with you. We had lots of happy memories in just one weekend."

Jake says, "We'll have to talk about it more later. I can't decide about this right now. I need to take time to think about it and figure out what is the best for both of us. You like Candy, right? You know I really like her, too? Meeting her has given me new life. I'll always love your Mom but I don't think she would want us to live our life feeling sad and lonely. I would like a chance to get to know Candy better. I'll have to figure that out also. We live a lot of miles apart."

"I know, Daddy. I was wishing that we could live closer so that we can spend more time with her. She's nicer than any other lady we know. When I give her hugs, she feels like my family. Her hugs feel like way Mommy used to hug me. I feel her love and love for her is in my heart. I just met her but I've never had feelings like this since Mommy went to heaven."

Jake says, "I'm glad you shared your feelings with me David. For an eight-year-old, you know how to express yourself very well. Let's go in now. There's not a busy crowd. Maybe, we'll have time to visit with Candy after all."

"I'm glad you listened and let me share with you. I'm almost nine years old, Daddy. I feel older sometimes. Okay, I'm hungry."

They get out of the car and enter the café. Jake makes a mental note about the "Part-Time Help Wanted" sign on the front door.

I'm working in the back office. Aunt Jen usually does the office work for me. The crowd has thinned out. Jerry and Marge came in again today to cover for Aunt Jen. They're cleaning up the dining area for me and then I've given them the rest of the day off to spend with their families. I do appreciate the sacrifice they made to help me last night and today. They're happy to earn the extra money but they appreciate the time they can spend with their family on the weekend.

Jake and David stand in front of the Deli counter eyeing the delicious looking food on display. They can't seem to make up their mind right away. They're both very hungry. Marge walks behind the counter and says, "Can I take your order?"

Jake asks, "What is today's special?"

She replies, "Meatball Sub is the special. It's been very popular with our customers today."

Jake asks David, "What do you think? Does that sound good to you?"

David responds, "I like spaghetti and meatballs. Does it taste like that?"

His daddy responds, "Probably. Usually, meatball sandwiches are made using meatballs with marinara sauce. Would you like to try it? We can share it. If you don't like it, we'll order something else for you."

David says, "Okay, I'll try it."

Jake orders a meatball sub, a glass of milk and a glass of sweet tea. He also asks Marge, "Can you please tell Candy that Jake and David are here and want to say goodbye."

She answers, "Sure, she's in the office. I'll be right back to fill your order and deliver it to your table." She gives David a box of crayons and a placemat.

They sit over in the corner by the window. It's the same table which Jake sat at when we first met. David goes to work coloring the picture on the placemat. This time it's a picture of Lacey. She's sitting up tall and looks regal with a sparkle in her eye. In the background is a scene of the lake with a clear blue sky.

David says, "Daddy, I love this picture of Lacey. I want to keep it to remember her always."

"That's okay with me! It's too bad that you don't have a gold crayon to match her beautiful golden coat."

"I have a gold crayon at home. I'll color her coat when I get home. I can color the rest of the picture for now,"

I told Marge that I want to take a break and join them for a few minutes. She's going to bring me a glass of sweet tea and she'll continue to cover the front counter. I suggested that she can take the rest of the day off in a half hour. She agreed, so I'm taking a few minutes to visit with Jake and David before they leave Happiness for home.

The clinking sound of the two glasses and two plates being placed on the table cause Jake and David to look up. They're surprised to see that I'm serving their food. I'm so glad that they're here.

With great excitement in his voice, David says, "Caaandyyy! I'm so happy to see you." He stands up and hugs me around my waist. I sit down beside him and hug him in return.

I ask, "Is it okay if I join you for a few minutes? I have time to take a break and sip a glass of sweet tea."

Jake splits the meatball sub to share with David and hands him a plate. They're both very hungry and start eating while I'm chatting away at them. They encourage me to stay at the table and visit before they must say goodbye.

I brought one of my business cards which I hand to Jake. I say, "If you have time and want to keep in touch, this is how you can contact me."

Jakes says, "That's a good idea." He reaches into his wallet and pulls out a business card. He also tells her, "Here is the info you'll need to contact us.

We'd love to keep in touch with you, Candy! If you ever travel my direction, please be sure to let us know. We have a big house with several extra rooms." He looks down and places his head on his forehead. "Ahem! What am I saying? Please, what I really mean is, if you can find some time for a trip to visit with us. We have an extra guest room. We look forward to spending fun time with you there."

I tell him, "I understand your need to take responsibility for your business. I also need to take responsibility for my business. After last night in the den, I thought a lot about a need to take a vacation. I was thinking that planning a getaway would give me a chance to sort through my thoughts and feelings. I don't want to leave Aunt Jenny and Darla alone without the help they'll need while I slip away."

"We would love to stay here longer and get to know you better. If you want to get to know us better, maybe you can drive out to our hometown. David will be out of school for spring vacation this week. I need to spend time in the office and make sure things are running smoothly. If you want to visit us this week, we surely can find time to entertain you and have lots of fun with you there. You can even bring Lacey with you because I have a big fenced yard. I know David will love that!"

David says, "Yes, I would love for you and Lacey to stay at our house during my spring vacation."

Chapter Seventeen
See You Later

"I would love to get to know you better. I adore both of you. It seems like I've known both of you all my life. Did you see the "Temporary Help Wanted" sign on the door? It's there because I want to hire extra help in the café. I want to be free for a getaway. At the time, I didn't dream about an invitation to your house. It sounds wonderful! Yes, if I can hire enough help for the café, I would absolutely love to visit with you at your house this week. Then, I won't have to worry about Aunt Jen pulling double duty at the B&B and café. She really needs to take time to rest and relax. She's been working hard for a lot of years. I would absolutely love to visit with you at your house, this week."

Jake says, "Speaking of hiring more employees...I gave your Aunt and Darla a gift before I left the Bed and Breakfast. I had a plan to give you a gift today, too. Now, you can use this freely as you see fit. It seems to me that the timing lines up with your desire to hire temporary staff." He takes out his checkbook and writes a $20,000 check payable to Candace Cotton.

I almost fell off my chair because of the shock of it. Tears of joy stream down my face. David reaches over with his little hands on my back and says, "Please don't cry, Candy! He gives me a kiss on my cheek and whispers, "Love you! Be happy!"

I laugh and tell David, "Thank you! I'm very happy! I love you, too!"

Jake and I look at each other, staring deeply once again. "Thank you, Jake for your generous gift.

Thank you for making this dream possible. I'll always be grateful."

Jake says, "The first time we met was here at the café. Now, we must say goodbye here at the Candy Cotton Café." He dries a tear from his eye but smiles with hope that we'll see each other again soon.

Jake tells David, "It's time for us to go now. You can take your picture and crayons with you to finish coloring it at home. If we leave now, we'll be home before your bed time."

Jake stands up and takes Candy's hand. He says, "Thank you for agreeing to visit with us this week. I hope with all my heart that you can work out the fine details. I'll be sure to have your bedroom freshly made up just in case. We can talk about a schedule of fun activities after you arrive. Let us know about Lacey? We'll enjoy taking a trip to the pet store and buy her new dishes, food and toys."

I stand up but I feel weak as though my knees can't hold me up. I walk with them to their car. I give David one last hug goodbye as he settles in to the backseat and then Jake and I embrace lovingly. I've never liked long goodbyes. We exchange a kiss and then I hear him whisper in my ear, "I love you!" My knees buckle and more tears flow but I gain the strength to whisper back, "I love you, too! Please take good care of yourself and David. I'll let you know if I can break free from here to make the trip to your town. I really look forward to seeing you both again. Until we meet again!" I don't want to let go but I pull away so that they can hit the road. I stand and watch them pull out of the parking lot. We wave goodbye and I see David blowing me a kiss. I laugh and blow a kiss back to him and another one for Jake. I watch them disappear as they travel down the main road that leads to the highway.

I return to the office. My first thought is a need to deposit my check for safe keeping. I know it's Sunday and the bank is closed but the night deposit box should be a safe place. Or, it might be better to wait until Monday. I want to take it home and share the news with Darla and Aunt Jen. For now, I place it securely in our office safe.

I let Marge and Jerry go home to be with their families. Now, I've got to finish the work that needs to be done for our supper meal. It's usually not very crowded on Sunday night. Most people around here want to be at home with their family. My usual Sunday night staff are scheduled to work tonight.

I want to check in with Aunt Jen. I send a brief text to her on her cell phone. "How are you doing? If you're up to a visit when I get home, I have some good news to share with you. How's Darla?"

She replies, "I'm feeling much better, now. Darla has taken good care of me and I've had a chance to rest and relax outside. The fresh air has been good for me. I guess I really need to slow down and not push myself so hard. Darla is doing fine. We have good news to share with you, too."

I send another text, "Why don't the two of you drive over to the café and eat supper here. Without guests at the B&B you're free to get out and about. It'll be my treat of course!"

Aunt Jen sends a message that reads, "We had a family reserve a couple of rooms this week. It seems that their children are on spring vacation. They have a little girl and a little boy. They'll arrive tomorrow. Darla and I will be there in just a few minutes. We'd love to eat supper at the café. Will you be able to join us?"

I reply, "It depends on how many customers that I'll need to take care of. As of now, it looks like I'll have time to join you. It'll be fun for the three of us to visit while we eat a meal together as a happy family. See you soon."

I secure the office and check on the dining area. My employees have arrived and I'm thankful to see that they've been working on their own to prepare for the supper hour. I individually thank each one of them. I also let them know that I will eat supper with my family here tonight. They're all happy to hear this news. They've seen me work long hard hours for a long time. All my employees encourage me to take the time for myself and enjoy.

Several families arrive for supper. I greet them at the door but I ask Jamie to seat them at their table and give them their menus. One of the young customers says, "Hello, my name is Georgia. I noticed the sign on your door. Where can I find an application to apply for a temporary job? I want to earn and save money for college classes. I just moved to Happiness a few weeks ago."

I reply, Hello, Georgia. I'm delighted to meet you. My name is Candy Cotton. I'm the owner of the café. Do you have time to walk back to the office with me? I'll give you an application. We'll take a few minutes to talk after I ask you a few questions. Then if you have questions, you can ask me. I'm anxious to hire a good experienced waitress that is willing to work odd days and hours."

"Yes, I'm here alone. I stopped in just to apply for the job. I met your cousin, Darla, at the college library. I was surprised when I saw your help wanted sign. She told me about your café but didn't mention that you were looking for temporary help."

I explain, "I just placed that sign on the door this morning. I haven't had time to tell her about it. She's going to be here soon. We're planning to eat supper here together as a family tonight."

We sit in the office while she fills out the application. We talk about where she lived before moving to Happiness. I ask, "What is your experience as a waitress?"

She replies, "Back in my hometown, I've worked as a waitress at several different restaurants since I was a teenager. I needed to earn money to assist my parents. They were having a struggle earning enough money to provide for my brother and me. I'm a hard worker and a quick learner. I'm impressed with your café. I'd love to work here. I'd really be happy if you give me a chance."

I ask, "Did you move here by yourself or did your family move here, too?"

She answers, "I moved here by myself to attend the local college. It has good reviews. Also, my Mom attended the college before she met my Dad."

I explain, "I'm planning to take a vacation this week. I haven't had one for a long time. I decided to hire temporary help that can fill in for me while I'm away. My Aunt will be coming here tonight as well. She also works at the café with me. You would answer to her. I'll introduce you tonight when she arrives with Darla."

She says, "Oh, great, it'll be great to see Darla again. She's given me a warm welcome to the college and to the town of Happiness."

Have you eaten supper yet? You're welcome to join us. You said you met Darla at the library? This meal will give both of you a chance to get to know each other better. You'll find that the people who live in Happiness are very friendly and family oriented."

She replies, "Thank you for the generous offer. I'm kind of broke right now. I can't afford to eat out."

I tell her, "It'll be my treat this time. I'd like to officially hire you to work part time for us here. Tomorrow, Monday, the café is closed. Can you start on Tuesday? If so, we'll decide with Aunt Jenny how to set up your position and work schedule properly. My Aunt Jenny doesn't know this yet, but I'll be gone on Tuesday and the rest of the week."

She says, "Thank you for giving me a chance to work for you here. I'm grateful to have a chance to earn the much-needed money for my education. I can start on Tuesday and look forward to meeting your Aunt tonight. Thank you for everything."

We walk back to the dining room. Everything is running smooth. Just as I expected there are only a few family dinners being served. Darla and Aunt Jenny have just walked through the door. Jamie is seating them at a table for four. Perfect!

Georgia and I join them at the table. I introduce her to Aunt Jenny. She says, "I'm delighted to meet you Georgia." I share with Aunt Jenny and Darla, "I invited her to join us for our family meal. She's new in town and I've just hired her part time to work here."

Darla is thrilled and says, "Oh, Georgia, I'm so happy for you. I think that you're going to like working here with my aunt and cousin. Welcome to Happiness!"

The ladies sit quietly while they read over their menus. Jamie strolls over and asks, "Are you ready to place your order?"

We're very hungry. We all place our meal orders. While Darla and Georgia are chatting quietly, I quietly chat with Aunt Jen. She asks, "When did you decide to hire a new waitress?"

"I decided this morning to advertise for part-time help. When you were sick this morning, I was concerned about not having enough staff to make it through a potentially busy day. I also recalled how you covered for me while I spent the day with Jake and David. I worried about you working too hard when you covered for me. I feel it's time to hire an extra waitress to help us out when the occasion arises."

"I'm feeling better and should be able to work at the café on Tuesday. It's a good thing right now that it's closed tomorrow. Will Georgia be available on Tuesday just in case?"

I reply, "Yes, I asked her. She said that she's available to start work on Tuesday. I need to tell you, though, I may not be available. That's part of the good news that I want to share with you and Darla."

She asks, "What's going on, Candy?"

"Jake and David invited me to join them in their hometown for a visit this week. I'm planning to take them up on their offer and that I'll see them again soon."

Chapter Eighteen
The Future Looks Bright

Jamie serves our meals. The food is delicious and we enjoy eating while we continue to chat and share news about our day. Darla and Georgia continue their discussion about their lives. I continue to chat with Aunt Jen.

I tell her, "After my wonderful time with Jake and David yesterday, I woke up this morning feeling the need for a getaway. I felt that getting away would give me a chance to sort out my thoughts and feelings. My heart felt like it would break with the thought of never seeing them again."

She asks with wide eyes, "So, instead of a getaway, you're planning to accept his invitation to visit them in their hometown?

I explain, "Yes. Jake and David ate lunch here before leaving town. Jake extended an invitation to me and Lacey to travel to their hometown this week. David is on spring vacation from school. They're both excited about the possibility that we can get to know each other better. We'll schedule a few fun activities and share time together at his house."

Aunt Jen says, "Oh, Candy. That does sound like a great opportunity for you. I believe you're making a wise choice. This time together will help you decide if you're really soulmates. I'll do whatever I can to help you figure out a way to make it happen. Fortunately, hiring Georgia today will increase your chances. Will you be leaving here tomorrow?"

"I know it's asking a lot of you. It's probably not fair to ask you at the last minute but I'm hoping we can work it out. I'd like to spend the whole week with them if possible. It would be great if I can leave here tomorrow. I'm already longing to be with them again. They've only been gone a few hours. I hope he'll call or text. I gave him a business card with my contact information. I'd like to know if they've arrived home safely."

Aunt Jen says, "Making plans at the last minute is difficult but not impossible. I'm okay and do not think your plan is a bad one. I encouraged you to take Saturday off from work. I also encourage you to take the week off for the same reason. If Jake is your soulmate you need to know. If you two have fallen in love, then you should be together. We often dream about living happily ever after. I'll be happy for you if that dream becomes a reality for you."

I tell her, "Thank you for your encouragement and support. I appreciate a chance to pursue my dream of being married and being a mom. It takes a lot of courage for me to pack up and leave the security of my home and life here. I feel a strong desire to do it for the sake of knowing for sure if Jake could be my Mr. Right. I could wait until he returns in the summer for vacation. I really want to be with both Jake and David. I enjoy their company and the family connection with them feels strong. I miss them and the happy feelings I had when they were here. Visiting with them in their hometown and learning more about them seems like the right thing for me to do. Thanks for letting me share all of this with you, Aunt Jen! You've been like a Mom to me for many years."

"I'm glad you feel comfortable sharing your thoughts and feelings with me. Just keep following your heart as well as your head. You've always been a smart young lady. I believe you should trust your instincts. I'm finished eating and ready to go home."

"I have more good news to share with you and Darla. I need to finish closing the café. I'll be back here in just a minute."

About an hour ago, all the customers left while we were busy eating and chatting. The employees completed their work and clocked out. It's just the four of us left in here now. I locked the front door and removed the "help wanted" sign from the door. Everything looks great! I still have a few loose-ends to tie up in the office.

After Georgia says goodbye, I ask Darla and Aunt Jen to join me in the office for a few minutes. I take Jake's check out of the safe and share the good news with them. They in turn share their good news with me. The three of us are overjoyed and grateful for Jake's life changing gifts to the Cotton Family. They tell me that they've deposited their checks at their banks already. Banks are closed on Sunday but they opted to use the night depository box. That's a lot of money sitting in the box but they are convinced it's safer there than in the house and the B&B.

I tell them, "I'll be sure to deposit my check in the bank tomorrow before I leave town. I think it will be okay to leave it in my safe here. We have a great security system. I also trust the people that live and work in this town. I'd love to share more about my $20,000 story and I would love to hear more about your stories. It's all very exciting!"

Darla says, "Jake gave me a gift to help me pay for my college classes."

Aunt Jen, says, "He gave me a gift to help with our Bed and Breakfast. I shared with him that I've thought about retiring. I told him that we had difficulty paying all the taxes this year."

I share, "He gave each of us a generous gift for different reason. He trusts us to spend it wisely and I'm sure we will. The gift he gave me today will assist me in hiring more employees so that we have more free time. Having more free time will be a great stress relief."

Aunt Jen asks, "Speaking of extra employees, will Georgia need on the job training on Tuesday?"

I reply, "She's had years of waitress experience. She's very smart. I think that she'll easily pick up on the way we do things here. I don't think she needs very much OJT. I don't want it to be a burden for you. Maybe, Jamie can help her throughout the day. She's scheduled to work on Tuesday. Jamie is one of my best employees. I feel confident that everything will work out great if you're feeling up to working in the office, too. I don't want you to push yourself too hard."

"Okay, I admit that I'm really tired right now. I look forward to getting home and into bed. We're expecting guests at the B&B this week. I'll want to enjoy our day from the café as well as greet our guests. Are we ready to leave here now?"

Darla says, "Yes, I'm ready to leave. I still have a few things to do tonight and in the morning before our new guests arrive."

Aunt Jen says, "Darla, I don't have a lot of energy but I'll do whatever I can to help you tonight and in the morning."

Darla says, "I'd like to see you get as much rest as you can tonight. If I still need help in the morning, maybe you'll feel better and more able to lend a hand. I don't want you to push yourself so hard either. We love you!

The three of them huddle in for a group hug. Aunt Jen says, "And I love you, too!" Darla and Aunt Jen leave the café and drive home. I drive close behind and we arrive at home at about the same time.

When I enter the kitchen, I notice Lacey is moping around looking lost. I'm sure she misses the love David and Jake gave her while they were here. I tell her, "We'll be with them again soon. We're going to take a road trip to visit with them at their house." I laugh and then I cry. I have mixed emotions.

Darla is scurrying around preparing the rooms that were reserved for this week. Aunt Jen has a cup of tea brewing in the kitchen while she builds a small fire in the den. The tea smells good and it's tempting to sit down and visit with her. I need to pack up clothes that I need for this week. I've never been away from Happiness for a whole week. I'm not sure what I need to pack. I'm sure it's safe to pack springtime clothes. I can always go shopping there if I forget to pack something.

While I'm trying to find my suitcase in the storage closet located in the basement, my phone rings and I answer it. It's David. I'm surprised of course because I thought Jake would call me first.

David says, "Hello, Candy. Daddy said it's okay for me to call you. He's still driving the car. He asked me to tell you that he'll call you when we arrive at our house. I'm using his phone because I want to talk to you before I fall asleep. I want to say goodnight. I hope to see you this week. Are you going to visit with us at our house?"

"I'm planning to visit with you. I'm going to pack up a few things in my suitcase tonight. I'm trying to make plans to leave here tomorrow morning or afternoon. I hope everything is going well for you and your daddy. I thought you would be home by now. Please tell your Daddy that stay awake until I hear from him. Hope you have sweet dreams, David."

David says, "Okay. I'll tell him. Hope you have sweet dreams, too. Goodnight!" David ends the call. I was anxious to hear that they made it home safe. I really imagined they should have arrived there by now. I don't want to worry but something doesn't seem quite right with this scenario.

I take the suitcase to my room and pack more than enough changes of outfits for the week. I pack both dress up and casual outfits as well as shoes and bags to match. I can feel butterflies in my stomach multiplying. I take a quick shower and get ready for bed. I make a trip downstairs in my robe to check on Aunt Jen and make myself a cup of tea. Darla finished the work she needed to do tonight. She's sitting and resting with Aunt Jen in the den.

I tell them, "I'm packed and ready for my trip tomorrow. I'm planning to take Lacey with me. David invited her, too! Taking Lacey on my trip will give you both a little more free time. Is there anything that I can do for either of you before I go to my room for the night? I spoke with David earlier because he called to say goodnight. He said that they're not home yet. He also said that his daddy will call me when they arrive at their house."

Aunt Jen says, "I can't think of anything that you can do. I'm ready for bed and I hope I'll sleep well tonight. I'll say goodnight to both of you. See you in the morning. Sleep well.:

Darla says, "Goodnight, Aunt Jen. Sleep well and feel better."

I also wish Aunt Jen a good night and sweet dreams.

Darla smiles at me and says, "No, I think I have everything under control right now. I also need to get a good night's sleep. Do you want me to leave the fire for you? You look like you might want a chance to relax in here, too."

"Yes, I'll finish drinking my tea and relax here for a few minutes. Goodnight and sleep well, Darla. I'll see you in the morning."

Darla says, "Goodnight, Candy! Sleep well." She goes upstairs to her room.

I'm alone with my thoughts now while waiting for Jake to call me.

Chapter 19
I'm Courageous

I'm exhausted and feeling very sleepy. The fire in the fireplace has burned down to a few flickering embers. The best thing for me to do is go on up to my room and get a good night's sleep. Because I've never driven to Springfield, I'll need to follow the GPS directions installed on my phone. I want to feel refreshed and alert while I'm driving on the highway.

I imagine, he'll be busy caring for David and unpacking the car when he arrives home. While stretched out on my bed, I send him a quick text, "I'm very sleepy and close to falling asleep. I'll text you again tomorrow morning around breakfast time. After I talked to David, I tried to stay awake but it's been a long exhausting day. I hope all is well with you. Look forward to hearing from you. Love, Candy"

I decide to turn on my alarm clock because I want to be up and dressed early. There are last minute preparations for the road trip that need my attention. My gift is waiting in the café safe for me to deposit it in the bank. I turn out all the lights and close my eyes. A mental list continues to grow as I try to turn off my mind and relax. I must get a good night's sleep.

I just barely doze off when I hear my phone chime. I pick it up off the night stand and check to see if it's Jake. He sent a text, "Goodnight, Candy. Sorry for the delay. We just arrived home safe and sound. We faced a couple of unforeseen obstacles. I'll be in touch with you in the morning. Sweet Dreams. Love, Jake"

I wake up out of a sound sleep with both the alarm ringtone and the chime on my phone. I hit the snooze button on my alarm but check my phone again.

Jake's message reads, "We really need to talk. Please call me when you are up. I look forward to seeing you here but I'm concerned for your safety. David sends his love and hugs. Love, Jake"

I'm still so sleepy, my eyes can't focus on typing a reply. While leaving my phone on the nightstand, I reset my alarm for another hour. I want to be rested when I hit the road. Although I can hear Darla and Aunt Jen prepare their breakfasts, the sound is not enough to entice me to rise and shine yet.

I fall into a deep sleep and wake up feeling refreshed before my alarm rings. Feeling energized and excited I bounce out of bed and get dressed. I find Darla and Aunt Jen sitting outside on the deck enjoying a cup of coffee in the early morning breeze. I step out and say, "Good Morning. Is it okay if I join you?"

Darla says "Sure, I'm just taking a break from my morning chores. Our new guests will arrive in a few hours."

Aunt Jen replies, "Of course. How are you feeling today?"

She answers, "I'm feeling anxious. After I eat breakfast, I need to call Jake. In an early morning text, he stated that they 'faced unforeseen obstacles". I wonder what he meant. He also stated that he's "concerned" for my safety. I'm not sure if I'll travel today or not,"

Aunt Jen says, "Oh? I hope that everything will work out for you. Please let me know if there's anything I can do."

"I'm going to pour a cup of coffee and get a plate for a cinnamon roll. Do either of you want a refill? Or a roll?"

Both Darla and my Aunt agree to a coffee refill. I take their mugs in with me. After I place a roll on a plate, I pour three mugs of coffee and place them on a serving tray. When I reach the back door, Darla helps by removing their mugs from the tray. It's a beautiful morning. Perfect spring setting for eating breakfast on the deck. Lacey is out rolling in the grass and chasing bugs. I make a mental note to give her a bath before she gets in my car today. That's a good plan whether I travel today or not. Right after I call Jake, I'll decide for sure whether I want to do it or if I should take him to Peggy's Pet Store. She does a beautiful job bathing and brushing her.

I'm really lost in thought while Aunt Jen and Darla are chatting. I hear Darla faintly calling my name. Suddenly, I realize Aunt Jen is also calling my name. They're both trying to get my attention. My phone is ringing in the kitchen. I forgot to carry it with me.

I take the tray with my cup and plate back to the kitchen which is on the way to my phone. I answer it and hear Jake's voice ask me, "Are you okay? I really need to talk to you. Is this a good time?"

I feel like I'm out of breath but I answer, "Yes, I'm okay. Let me get settled in the den. I'll have a little more privacy there now." I sit in the recliner and say, "Okay, go ahead. What happened on your trip yesterday? Why are you concerned for my safety?"

Jake says, "I hope you it won't view it as a serious problem but I want you to be forewarned. I don't want you to feel pressured to make the trip. I'm concerned you might feel threatened while you're here.

You may decide not to visit with us after I tell you our story."

"What's happening, Jake? Tell me please?"

Jake answers, "We stopped at a truck stop off the highway for supper and a break to stretch our legs. Someone at the truck stop confronted me saying, "Hey, I saw you on the TV. He was creating a scene which caused David and me a lot of fear. We decided to get back in the car and find a different place for our supper. When I pulled out of the parking lot, several cars sped up behind me and followed us for a few miles. I took a turn off the highway to lose them. We still feel shaken by that incident. I've been in the spotlight a lot for many years. I imagine if it scares David and I that it might scare you too. I'm not worried about you on the highway while you're driving here. Once the paparazzi sees us together in Springfield, they might give you unwanted attention."

"I admit that does sound pretty scary. You'll have to teach me about disguises. What happened to your disguises last night?"

"Before David fell asleep in the backseat, he removed his hat and sunglasses. I forgot to put them back on. He's just so cute, he always gets lots of attention. Turns out someone saw him with me on the TV and made the connection."

"That's too bad and very sad. Poor little David. I can imagine how scared he was with people chasing you and speeding on a busy highway."

"I always do my best to protect him but this time I failed. There are stories on TV and in the newspaper with photos that were taken by someone in the crowd. I'm not confident in my ability to protect you. I want us to enjoy touring downtown Springfield but now I'm not sure it'll be safe for you and David to be out and about. This is one reason I feel stressed out all the time. We really got spoiled by hiding out in Happiness."

I ask, "What do you think I should do? Do you still want me to visit with you there? I'm willing to take the risk but I don't want to cause you any grief."

He replies, "Yes, David and I really miss you. I would like for you to spend the week with us. But you need to make the decision regarding what is best for you regarding your safety." He takes a deep breath, pauses and says, "Oh, there's one more thing."

I ask, "What? I hope it's not worse than what you've already shared with me."

He responds, "I just didn't see this coming either. I let David use my phone to call Nanny. While he was talking to her, he shared the story about meeting you and the fun time we had. He told me afterwards, Nanny is upset and crying like her heart is broken."

He continues, "She was at the house when we arrived home. I hired her to be a live-in Nanny after my wife passed. I noticed she was visibly upset and questions were flying. I hadn't realized that she was so emotionally attached to us. She expressed jealousy and disappointment in the fact that I invited you to stay in our guest room."

I gasp and react surprised, "Oh, no, Jake! I don't want to cause any problems for you and David. Maybe, I shouldn't plan on staying at your house. I still want to see you and visit with you and David. I'll make a reservation at a hotel close to your house."

He says, "I really don't think that she'll cause you any harm but it would be best to avoid her until she has a chance to accept the facts. I set the record straight about my lack of romantic feelings for her. She walked out and said that she would pick up her things in the morning. She came in this morning, packed up all her things and told David goodbye. He seemed devastated at first and asked me a lot of questions. He seems to be okay now. But I'll have to hire a new Nanny before school starts next week."

I share, "I'm willing to spend time with him while you're at work at least during the week that I'll be there."

He asks, "Do you still want to visit with us after I shared these stories with you? I'll make a reservation for you at the hotel for at least the first night. Then you can decide after that if you want to stay in the guest room."

I remind him, "If I stay in a hotel, it will be better to leave Lacey at home. You did say I can bring her to your house. What is your opinion about Lacey now?"

He answers, "Oh, yes, Lacey?! I'm sorry. In all the confusion, she slipped my mind. I think David has his heart set on you bringing Lacey. I'm looking forward to seeing her again, too. It's up to you. It's important to me that you feel safe and secure."

I say, "This is a totally new adventure for me. I'm willing to be courageous and take risks because that's the way I want to live my life. Life is short and I don't want it to pass me by. I'm going to follow my heart and accept your invitation to stay in the guest room. I'll bring Lacey and plan on caring for David there at your house while you're at work. I assume you have a good security company watching your house. Besides, we'll have Lacey guarding and protecting us. I feel confident that we'll be okay. I packed my suitcase last night. I only have a few more things to do before I can leave Happiness and head to Springfield. I have some business to take care of first. Is it okay with you if I plan to arrive before the supper hour?"

He laughs and says, "Yes, Yes and Yes! Arriving before the supper hour and bringing Lacey, staying in the guest room all sounds good to me. I know David will be thrilled. I learned something new about you. You're courageous and willing to take risks in search of what makes your heart happy. I really admire that about you."

I say, "I better say goodbye for now. I need to check off my mental to-do-list as soon as possible."

"Okay, Candy, please call or text me before you leave Happiness. Goodbye for now."

Chapter Twenty

Welcome to Springfield

I'm moving forward with my travel plans now that Jake and I have connected. First chore on my to-do-list is to call Peggy's Pet Store. I have their number stored on my phone. Peggy is a good friend and Lacey is a regular in the grooming department during the summer. The more time she spends outside the more she needs special grooming care. We just don't have the time to bathe her very often. We pay Peggy to do it for us.

I call the store and ask to speak with her. She's not in the store now but the store manager assures me that there is groomer available to take care of her now. With that, I take off with Lacey in the backseat of my car. We drive to the pet store and take Lacey back to the groomer. She says, "I can finish bathing her, blow drying and brushing her coat within the hour. Did you want her toenails trimmed? I can do that for you, too."

I say, "Yes, that sounds great. I'll be here in the store shopping for a few items for her while you're doing that. Her name is Lacey and my name is Candy."

She says, "Don't worry, I've got lots of experience at this job. I'll take good care of her for you."

I walk around the store with a shopping cart picking out several new items that I can take on the trip for her. A lot of toys are worn out from playing hard with them. I'll buy her a new Frisbee and ball. Ah, I imagine it will be great to have a new bed, water dish, food dish and her favorite food. I like this new collar and matching leash. I should apply a flea and tick repellant, too. If I must stop off the highway to walk her, there's no telling what kind of brush or trees we'll encounter. Better to be safe than sorry. If she needs anything while we're in Springfield, I imagine they have at least one pet store.

I pay for Lacey's new supplies and notice the clock on the wall. It's lunchtime and I'm hungry. I walk back to the groomer. I tell her, "I need to run a couple of errands. Is it okay if I leave Lacey here for a few minutes beyond the hour you estimated? I'll try to be back before then but just in case. Will you be okay if you wait until I can return to pick her up?"

"Yes, we have a kennel or a play area that she will be safe in until you return. It would be best for her sake if you pick her up as close to an hour as possible."

I say, "Here's my business card with my cell phone number. Please call me if you need me to return sooner. It shouldn't take very long for me to run to the bank and grab a sandwich to eat for lunch."

She says, "Sounds like a good plan. See you later."

I take my shopping bags with me to the car and place them in the trunk. First stop is the café. It's closed today but I think I'll fix a club sandwich from the food stored in the deli meat cooler. I open the safe and locate my gift from Jake. I hide it securely in my purse. After I lock up the safe, I pour sweet tea in a to-go cup, grab my sandwich bag and secure the front door. Check! Next stop is the bank where I deposit my check in my business account. Check! Next on my to-do-list is filling up my car with gas, checking the tires. It's the same station that regularly repairs and services my car for me. Check!

I drive back to the pet store and park but notice I still have a few more minutes to wait for Lacey's grooming to be complete. I eat my sandwich in the car and feel refreshed by the delicious cold sweet tea. Ah, I return to the grooming department to pick up Lacey. She says, "Great! Our work is done here. My assistant is just about to tie a pretty pink bow around her neck." I laugh joyfully and pull out my cell phone to take a quick snap of how great she looks. I send the pic in a text to Jake and ask him to share it with David for fun. I pay for them for a job well done. Lacey and I get in the car and drive back to the B&B.

I'm glad it's not wet and muddy today. I locate and pack up a couple of Lacey's favorite toys from her box. She'll have something familiar to cuddle up with in her new bed. I scurry upstairs to pack my makeup bag. Also, I quickly pack my toothbrush and other personal needs. Darla is down the hall giving a tour to our new guests. I try not to bother them but I want to say goodbye.

I walk quietly down the hall and quickly whisper in her ear, "I love you Darla. Take care of yourself and Aunt Jen, please." The new guests are checking out the view on the balcony. I quickly add, "Please keep in touch with me. You can call or text me at any time. left two envelopes on the kitchen counter by the coffee pot. One for you and Aunt Jen. I wrote down Jake's contact information from his business card and I drew a map and wrote down the driving directions to Springfield. I'll try to text a picture or two. I'll see you later."

We exchange a quick goodbye hug and she says, "Stay safe. I love you. I'll keep in touch. See you later. Have lots of fun."

I take all my travel bags out of my room and take them out to my car. I pack it all away in the trunk. I move Lacey's new bed to the back seat where she will lay down while I'm driving down the highway. I spot Aunt Jen down on the beach. She's relaxing in a lounge chair and petting Lacey. I'm glad Lacey did not venture into the water while I was busy packing.

I walk down to the beach to say goodbye to Aunt Jen. I feel powerful emotions stirring inside me. I don't like goodbyes. I tell her instead, "I'm going to take Lacey with me to Springfield now. I left a note for you in the kitchen with all of Jake's contact information along with a map showing the location of Springfield and driving directions. I'll see you again at the end of the week."

She stands up and gives me a goodbye hug. She says, "Have a safe trip there and back. I'll miss you. I love you. Hope you know that? Good luck in Springfield. Let's keep in touch while you're gone, okay?"

"You can call or text me any time of the day or night. I'll text a couple of pictures to you, too. Please take good care of yourself. If you're not feeling up to working on Tuesday, please ask one of our employees for help. Hopefully everything will run smooth while I'm gone. This a new adventure for me. I love you, Aunt Jen!" I dry tears from my eyes. I'm going to miss everything and everyone that is so near and dear to me here in Happiness. But I'll be back soon.

I say, "I'll see you later." I turn and walk toward the car with Lacey following me. Lacey settles in on the backseat and I start up the car. Aunt Jen waves goodbye as I back out of the parking lot in front of the B&B."

I drive off slowly while I mentally rethink my to-do-list. A short distance down the road, I stop and pull over to the side of the road. I just recalled a promise to Jake. I send a text to him, "I'm leaving Happiness now. I'll see you in a few hours. I'll probably have to take at least one stop between here and there. I'll need to walk Lacey and seek comfort for myself."

He replies, "Thanks for letting us know. Please let us know when you're in Springfield. I wish you a safe and happy trip."

Then I recall, I forgot to bring the thermos of water for Lacey and me. I also made a thermos of sweet tea for myself. I drive the short distance back to the B&B. I prepared the thermoses but accidentally left them on the table on the back deck. I slip out of the car and grab them quickly. I don't want to disturb anyone. I'm on my way to Springfield again.

My mind is clear now and I feel refreshed and alert. I drive to the highway and head in the direction of Springfield. I drive for about an hour and a half and decide to make a stop at a roadside park. There's a pet area for Lacey. There are maps and other brochures advertising a variety of tourist attractions. I take a map and several brochures advertising fun things that we might do while I'm in Springfield. I find Lacey's new water dish in the trunk. I take a few minutes to pour water in the dish and let her have a drink. I'm also feeling thirsty so I pour a cup of sweet tea. I drink it down and then we settle back into the car. Breathing a lot easier after taking in a breath of fresh air and stretching my legs.

Another hour and a half later, I see the highway sign for Springfield. At this point, I check the GPS signals on my phone. I place it in the dock on my dashboard. Once I know for sure that I'm in the right area of the city, I pull off into a parking lot. I call Jake and tell him, "I made it to Springfield. Now, I hope I can find your house. I have my GPS on my phone. I must be pretty close to your house."

He asks, "Where are you now?"

I look up at the building and see the sign for a hotel. I laugh because this is probably the hotel we talked about earlier today. I tell him, "I just happened to pull into the Springfield Luxury Hotel parking lot to make this call." I hear him laughing.

He says, "My house is located several miles from there." Is your GPS signal accurate? If not, please wait right there. David and I will be over to escort you the rest of the way. I don't want you to get lost in this big city."

I reply, "Ok, I'll sit here and wait for you to rescue me. The parking lot and building are lit up big time. I've never seen so many lights in one parking lot and on one building." We both laugh!

While I sit, and wait, I talk to Lacey and soothe her with a few strokes down the middle of her back. She's not used to being stuck in a car for several hours. She slept most of the way which was good for both of us. The brochures are sitting on the front seat. I pick out a couple to browse through just to keep busy while I'm waiting.

Fortunately, Jake parks his car a few spaces down. I get out and meet him halfway. We greet each other with a hug. There's an electrical charge between us that seems to express relief that I made it there safely. Also, big smiles are shared. He says, "Just follow me and we'll be at my house in a short time. This really is a beautiful hotel, isn't it?"

"Yes, 'luxury' hotel is right. I imagine that I wouldn't be able to afford a room here for the night." He walks me back to my car and then he hurries back to his car where David is waiting." I wait for him to back out of his parking space. I back out and follow close behind. We arrive in front of a mansion size estate where he parks his car in a long-curved driveway. I pull in behind him and park my car. I'm feeling a bit dazed by the size of their driveway. Their house appears to be just as luxurious as the Springfield Luxury Hotel.

Jake and David sprint to my car with big smiles. They happily greet Lacey and me. Like a true gentleman, Jake opens my car door and offers his hand. David is helping Lacey exit the backseat.

Staring deeply in my eyes, Jake says, "We first met and had to say goodbye at the Candy Cotton Café in Happiness. I'm so glad you accepted our invitation to visit here on spring break. When I left Happiness, I really wasn't sure if you wanted to see me again. I really want to know more about you."

Staring back at him, our eyes lock once again. I say, "I wouldn't have driven all those miles from Happiness, if I didn't want to know more about you. Spring break is a good time for me to learn more about you and David. I'm very happy to accept your invitation. I look forward to a fun filled week at your beautiful home here in Springfield."

He embraces me, kisses me on my forehead and says, "Welcome to Springfield! But don't forget, we plan to return for a summer vacation in Happiness where we'll be together again at the 'Candy Cotton Café'."

Epilogue

... To Be Continued.

Candy, Jake and David will enjoy spring break in Springfield. They'll make plans to meet again in Happiness during a summer vacation. David asked his Dad to return to the Cotton Family Bed and Breakfast. He dreams of having more fun boating on the lake as well as other activities.

Jake spends time in his office and successfully takes care of pressing issues. He doesn't like the news reporters stalking him. He wants to have a normal and secure life with his son as well as Candy.

Candy's parents provided well for her as a child growing up. She certainly didn't see or experience luxury like Jake provides for David. Jake described his weekend in Happiness to be a new adventure. Candy's visit in Springfield will prove to be over the top.

About the Author

I'm a wife, Mom of 3, Mom-in-law, Gramma to 7, sister, aunt, with cousins by the dozens. I love spending quality time with my family, friends & extended family. We currently reside in Nebraska.

My pen name, Lola, was created by merging the first two letters (LO) of my name with the first two letters (LA) of my husband's name. He is my proofreader, encouragement and support.

I've always loved WORDS! I appreciate puns, word games & creative writing. I've enjoyed writing original music with Christian lyrics, Christian poems and other poems in the past. This year, I felt overwhelmed with passion to write my first novel, 'Love Grows in Omaha'. My 2nd book is a sequel, "Young Family's Autumn. Blessings". I plan on writing more stories about the Young Family. I'm currently in the process of writing more love stories and children's books. My favorite stories are about love, family and commitment. I enjoy movies and books in the romantic comedy genre.

My hobbies/interests include singing Karaoke as a member of an online community, camping in our RV, picnics by the lake, baking, photography, creating art, listening to relaxation music and lots more. These hobbies help me cope with multiple health challenges daily. I'm also hearing and vision impaired. My favorite flowers are pink sweetheart roses. I wish you all love, peace and joy.

More Books from Lola's Bookshelf:

www.amazon.com/author/lola

- Love Grows in Omaha
- Young Family's Autumn Blessings

www.ingramcontent.com/pod-product-compliance
Lightning Source LLC
Chambersburg PA
CBHW070930130626
46555CB00001B/364